Sparks in the Darkness

Blue Moon Investigations

Book 19

A Novella

Steve Higgs

Text Copyright © 2021 Steven J Higgs

Publisher: Steve Higgs

The right of Steve Higgs to be identified as author of the Work has been asserted by him in accordance with the Copyright, Designs and Patents Act 1988

All rights reserved.

The book is copyright material and must not be copied, reproduced, transferred, distributed, leased, licensed or publicly performed or used in any way except as specifically permitted in writing by the publishers, as allowed under the terms and conditions under which it was purchased or as strictly permitted by applicable copyright law. Any unauthorised distribution or use of this text may be a direct infringement of the author's and publisher's rights and those responsible may be liable in law accordingly.

'Sparks in the Darkness' is a work of fiction. Names, characters, businesses, organisations, places, events, and incidents either are the product of the author's imagination or are used fictitiously. Any resemblance to actual persons, living, dead or undead, events or locations is entirely coincidental.

Dedication

I feel a need to dedicate this book to the Blue Moon Investigations team. Tempest, Amanda, and Jane. Big Ben too for obvious reasons and let's not forget Tempest's parents, plus Bull and Dozer, his loyal dachshunds, Frank, Poison, Patience, and many others.

Did I invent them all? Or were they out there just waiting to find the right mind to bring them to life? I believe the answer depends entirely upon one's outlook on life. One day they were not in my head, the next they were.

Many years and several adventures later, they are part of me and always will be.

Table of Contents

A New Entry on the Chart. Thursday, October 12th 1812hrs

Royal Targets. Thursday, October 12th 1927hrs

Two Sides of the Same Team. Thursday, October 12th 1934hrs

A Royal Arrival. Thursday, October 12th 2001hrs

A Crazy Plan. Thursday, October 12th 2012hrs

The Younger Brother. Thursday, October 12th 2026hrs

Fire. Thursday, October 12th 2048hrs

Fire at Will. Thursday, October 12th 2055hrs

Evidence. Thursday, October 12th 2102hrs

Stalemate. Thursday, October 12th 2117hrs

It Doesn't Add Up. Thursday, October 12th 2130hrs

Epilogue. Thursday, October 12th 2258hrs

Author's Notes

What's next for the Blue Moon Crew?

Patricia and Barbie

Miss May and Chelsea

Patricia and Barbie: Arriving in New York

Miss May and Chelsea: Visiting Time

Patricia and Barbie: Two Sides of the Same Problem

Miss May and Chelsea: Heading to the Crime Scene

Patricia and Barbie: My Ego Is Bigger Than Yours

A New Team

On the Trail

Luggage Legends

Chased Again

What's in the Box?

Dinner and a Clue

The Man with the Money

Hatchet Men

Dirty Cop

A Secret No One Knows

Rugged Tires

Wolf

New Player

The Sting

Riding Pillion

Epilogue

Author's notes by Steve Higgs

Apple Orchard Cozy Mystery by Chelsea Thomas

More Books by Steve Higgs

Free Books and More

A New Entry on the Chart. Thursday, October 12th 1812hrs

I had to fight to stop the yawn that was threatening to split my head in two. The phone was ringing, insistently demanding I answer it. Yet even though I could pick it up and thumb the green button to connect the call, there was no way I could speak until I wrestled my fatigue under control.

Worried the caller might ring off if I let it go to voicemail, I touched the green button anyway.

A second ticked by as the caller waited for someone to speak. My jaw was still wide open, and I considered using both hands to force it shut.

'Hello?' a woman's voice rang through loud and clear. As my yawn finally subsided, I noted the clear, precise nature of the woman's accent. More correctly, I should say that her voice was without an accent, which is to say I heard no regional markers to place her from the west or the north or from a particular county. Rather, she just sounded posh to my ears, her upbringing one that might have involved private schools and Bentleys.

I was filling in a lot of blanks with silly imagined scenarios as I fought to get my teeth aligned so I could finally speak.

'Hello?' the woman repeated herself. 'Is there anyone there?'

'Yes, sorry,' I blurted. 'This is Jane Butterworth. Good evening and welcome to the Blue Moon Paranormal Detective Agency. How may I help you?'

'Is this call being recorded?' she asked, the question direct and demanding.

'Um, no,' I lied, turning off the recorder I habitually use.

I heard the woman exhale. 'Very well. My name is Detective Inspector Munroe. I am calling you from Buckingham Palace.'

'Buckingham Palace?' I questioned. 'Where the Queen lives?'

'The Queen is not in residence and rarely stays in Buckingham Palace,' the detective replied matter-of-factly. 'Neither is her majesty a factor in the matter at hand. I require …' the woman fell silent, giving me the impression she was wrestling with how to frame what she wanted to say.

This is not all that unusual in my line of work. As you probably gathered from the title of the firm, we specialise in paranormal investigations. Blue Moon was started by my boss, though I should probably refer to him as my colleague now. I am one of three detectives working at the agency. We have an office on Rochester High Street just a stone's throw from the cathedral. I came to the firm as an assistant to do the general administration tasks. However, after dabbling in a case because there was no one else to tackle it, I was swiftly promoted, and now get my own cases.

Before the police officer could speak again, I tried to finish her sentence. 'You have unexplainable events at the palace, and you need to hire a specialist who can be quiet and discreet.'

I got to hear DI Munroe sigh with relief. 'Yes, exactly that. Discretion is paramount in this matter.'

'Can you tell me what has occurred?' I begged.

Honestly, I expected her to regale me with a story of a ghost or a mysterious noise in the walls. Given that everything we deal with fell somewhere on the weirdometer, you can imagine how rarely I hear something that surprises me.

However, when she began explaining her problem, I was forced to interrupt. 'I'm sorry, you have a what?' I couldn't help but ask.

'A dragon,' DI Munroe repeated her previous words. 'At least, it flies and breathes fire, and I don't know what else to call it.'

Right. A dragon.

Swapping my phone from right hand to left, I crossed the office to the wall where we have a chart. Tempest – my boss – created it one night as a bit of fun. On the chart are our three names and beneath each are rows which list various creatures. There are ghosts, vampires, werewolves, pixies … you name it, and you can bet someone has called us to investigate one at some point. I was behind on werewolves, failing to score even one case yet, and Amanda was the only one who could claim to have been called to solve an alien-based mystery.

However, I took the handy pen set next to the chart and added a new row, writing the word dragon and putting a big tick under my name.

'Am I correct to assume you would like me to come now?' I checked.

DI Munroe replied instantly. 'Of course, Miss Butterworth … Is it Miss?' she asked, checking my marital status.

I almost told her that I'm actually a mister, but revealing my true gender when I am dressed and acting as Jane would do me no favours, so I brushed the question to one side.

'Jane will do. I shall leave immediately. How do I gain access to the palace? Is there a way in with my car?'

I listened intently, switching on the recorder again to catch her instructions as she relayed where I needed to go and how to avoid getting shot by the soldiers guarding the palace gates.

With the call ended and my car keys in my hand, I checked the office front door was secure and went out the back. I was going to Buckingham Palace.

Royal Targets. Thursday, October 12th 1927hrs

DI Munroe called me before I arrived, anxious to check on my progress. Consequently, she met me at the gate when I revealed I was only a few minutes from arriving. It made getting through the gate easy at least.

'Nice car,' she commented, sliding into the passenger seat of my Aston Martin to guide me through the palace grounds.

'It was a gift,' I admitted. I could never afford to buy such an extravagant car, not least because it was one of the stunt models made for the James Bond Movie, *The Living Daylights*, and still had all the secret buttons and devices on it. Not that the machine guns fired real bullets, they were just props, but it was fun to know I could press a button and have them pop up from the bonnet.

Munroe showed me where to park and started to fill me in on her problem.

'It started more than a week ago.'

'A week?' I questioned, amazed they had let it go on for so long.

'I didn't know what it was at the time.' She took a breath and plunged on. 'We found a body. It was one of the soldiers. A young private in the Grenadier Guards by the name of Karl Matthewson. He completed his two-hour watch and was relieved, but failed to return to the guard house. When the soldiers went looking for him, they found his charred remains. He was still clutching his rifle but hadn't managed to get a shot off.'

I stayed silent, noting everything she said in my head because she refused to let me record her or even write anything down.

'I was called at that point. I have quarters in the grounds of the palace,' she explained. 'It was ... is my job to investigate, but I will unhappily admit I have no idea what happened to the man. He wasn't near a source of fire, and I am not willing to believe in self-combustion.'

A memory surfaced, jolting me to focus on it. Months ago, we had a case where a man had self-combusted. We investigated on behalf of the family and there were other reports at the time that led us to believe there was a person messing around with fire.

Not your standard arsonist or pyromaniac though, this was something different. This was ... magical almost, like there was a person who could create, control, and manipulate fire. The trail went cold, and the case remained unsolved.

So far.

I dragged my thoughts back to the present because DI Munroe was still talking.

'After three days of expert opinion, forensic examination, and painstaking investigation, I had achieved nothing, but then one of the soldiers spotted something inside the palace grounds.'

I kept quiet, desperate to ask questions, but unwilling to interrupt her.

'There was a figure on the roof. Lance Corporal McKinnon's report states that it was a black figure with glowing orange eyes. He also said it had wings, though when I pressed him, he admitted he couldn't be sure about the last part. His words were corroborated by Guardsman Bartlet who was with him. They challenged it and raised the alarm before giving chase. They have a quick reaction force here at all times – it's a standard military thing apparently. The QRF as they call themselves, deployed within seconds, swarming the palace in a bid to cut off the intruder.'

'They didn't catch it,' I supplied, finding myself drawn into her tale.

'No,' she agreed. 'But with pressure from the palace to resolve this issue, and the press sniffing around because the family of the dead soldier are demanding answers, I gave up trying to do this myself and called you.' We were out of my car and walking across the moonlit palace grounds on our way to get inside when DI Munroe abruptly stopped moving.

I turned to face her to find her staring right at me. I guess she felt this part of her story required eye to eye contact so I would know how serious she was.

'The soldiers caught up to the ... thing on the roof. It was less than fifty yards from the Queen's bedroom. They opened fire when it disobeyed their challenge and vanished into the shadows. When they saw it again a few seconds later, they resumed firing.'

'They shot it?' I questioned, wondering what I was doing here if the thing they wanted my advice on was already dead.

'The bullets had no effect.' DI Munroe looked scared as she retold her story. 'According to the after-action report – that's what the soldiers call it – the ... dragon smashed through a window and set the curtains on fire, torching the room it went into so the soldiers could not follow.'

I could feel my own pulse rising, the startling nature of this case causing a creeping sense of self-doubt and worry to spread like chilled water through my veins.

'The soldiers were unsure what to do at that point. They never go inside the palace, and I think they hesitated before smashing windows in an adjacent room so they could follow. When they did, they discovered another body, this time one of the palace stewards. He was in the hallway outside the room the dragon broke in through. Wrong place at the wrong time. The QRF fanned out, going room to room as they attempted to find the beast. It was a mercy it didn't get to the members of the royal family currently in residence or ... well, you can imagine the headlines if someone broke in and killed the heir to the throne.'

I could indeed, but had a question. 'Who is in residence?'

'Since that second attack, almost no one. There were senior figures here, including the heir to the throne who was in London to host a big event for one of his charities. He was removed to a safer location within hours of the first incursion. Most of the others left shortly thereafter. Only one is still here, Lord Edward Chamberlain, second son of Duke Westborough. The duke is twelfth in line to the throne after Prince Charles, his sons, and Prince Charles' grandchildren. That makes Lord Chamberlain technically fourteenth in line to the throne, but he is far enough down the peerage that he doesn't get any special protection.'

'He is still here despite the attack?' I questioned.

DI Munroe nodded. 'Yes, he's quite cavalier about it and claims to see no danger. I know the palace wanted him to go but he declined. I am left with the belief he likes being the only royal in residence. Anyway,' she sucked in a deep breath, 'we've been digressing from the topic at hand, and we are yet to get to the best part.'

I cranked an eyebrow, wondering what was going to top the fire breathing dragon.

DI Munroe didn't make me wait. 'I am under orders to sew this up without the press ever knowing about it, but I'm not sure if that is going to be possible.'

'Why not?' I asked, my brow wrinkling with confusion.

DI Munroe pursed her lips and sighed deeply. 'Because of what happened next. The soldiers worked across the palace covering the top two levels in a systematic sweep. They did a great job at enormous personal risk and cornered the *dragon*,' it was clear from the way she said the word that she could scarcely believe it herself, 'as it made its way back to the roof. Then,' she sucked in a deep breath, 'it flew.'

'It flew?'

She nodded. 'That is what more than two dozen soldiers claim. It opened its wings and took off into the night sky. Two of the guardsmen opened fire, their rounds having no effect again. Mercifully, their commander ordered them to cease fire. He was rightly concerned the bullets would come to land in the grounds outside the palace – there are houses nearby and people going past at all times of the day and night.'

I did my best to summarise.

'We have a creature who is bulletproof, able to spew fire, and it can fly. Anything else?'

'Orange eyes,' DI Munroe reminded me. 'They estimated its height at about six feet and described it as able to defy gravity. I don't know what it is, but after the second attack ... well, let's just say I am under pressure to prevent a third incident from occurring.'

I watched the detective's face. There was something she wasn't telling me. Something about her personal motivations behind calling a paranormal investigator for help.

'Do you believe it is a dragon?' I sought to clarify.

The detective shrugged. 'I don't know what to think. I can get my head around the bulletproof and the flame thing, but the flying is hard to explain. Whatever my personal thoughts on the matter, my bosses will not entertain the idea that there is a supernatural creature plaguing the palace and if I suggest otherwise, I'll need a new job.'

There it was. That sense of something hidden.

'Why would they take your job away?' I challenged her. She was keeping something secret, and I hated not knowing all the parameters when I go into an investigation. It is like trying to read while looking through gauze.

DI Munroe sucked in a breath as she frowned and was about to give me a dismissive answer when I raised a knowing eyebrow and folded my arms. Her words caught in her throat, and I got to see her shoulders slump.

'It is not germane to the case,' she stated. 'But … look, this is a punishment post for me. You don't need to know the details, but if I don't sew this up quickly, or if I give my boss any just cause to question my ability, he will fire me.'

Enough said. There was something in her past that placed her on a bad footing. She came across as a little desperate and as she started walking again, I fell into step by her side.

It was time to see what clues she might have uncovered.

Two Sides of the Same Team. Thursday, October 12th 1934hrs

Inside the palace I got to see the evidence amassed thus far and saw DI Munroe in the light for the first time.

She was five feet and maybe four inches tall, wearing a trouser suit that hid her slender figure and a collared shirt unbuttoned at the top. Her ash-blonde hair was cut into a bob at the same length as her jaw which to me made her head look a bit like a mushroom. I guessed her age to be somewhere in her mid-thirties and she wore no jewellery, not even a ring. Whether she was unmarried or divorced was not a subject I needed to bring up.

She had a large office dedicated to her needs in the basement of the palace. Crime, as you might imagine, was next to non-existent, and I got why she referred to her position as a punishment. It would be hard to shine when there were no crimes to solve and every opportunity to mess up in a high-profile manner if she missed anything that did happen. I was curious to hear what she might have done to earn such a reprimand, but like she said, it was not germane to my visit.

The photographs of the two victims, however, were. They were hard to look at. Behind Guardsman Matthewson's body was a shadow. Or, rather, it was whatever the opposite of a shadow is called. Where the flame hit him, it splayed out to leave a soot mark on the wall and a man shaped hole in the middle of the soot where the wall was mostly untouched.

'Whatever our 'dragon' is using, it burns hot,' remarked DI Munroe, standing next to me as she showed me what she had so far. 'The forensic guys are still analysing it. So far they can tell me what it isn't.'

'What isn't it?'

'A standard accelerant a person can buy off the shelves. Their best guess so far is that it is something organic.'

'Organic,' I repeated her word. 'As in naturally occurring?' Oh, yeah, this was right up there on the weirdometer.

I got a sort of shrug from her – like she said, the boffins were working on it.

A knock on the door preceded a man in uniform entering. He was one of the soldiers, a man in his late twenties with a serious set to his face. He was over six feet tall, and handsome with a nice smile which he turned on me.

'Good evening,' he met my eyes. 'Captain Raef Duncan at your service.' He extended his hand which I shook. I guess something in the back of his head told him my hand was significantly bigger than he expected because his features froze, just for a second, as he looked down at my manly knuckles and back up at my face.

The two things didn't fit.

It's the hardest part of crossdressing and pretending to be a girl. I can change my voice, wear a wig and girl clothes, then use makeup to hide the rest. However, there is just no way to get around the fact that I have size ten feet and man-sized hands.

If Captain Duncan suspected anything, he was astute enough to keep it to himself.

'This is Jane Butterworth,' DI Munroe took care of the introduction. 'She is here to consult on our fiery problem.'

The soldier's serious expression returned.

'You called in outside help?'

'Whatever that thing is, it killed one of your men, Raef. You should be working with me on this.'

The soldier frowned at the detective. 'I am working with you, Cassandra. However, looking for clues and treating this like a criminal act is ridiculous.'

'You think this is a supernatural creature?' I asked, jumping into the conversation.

He swung his face around to pierce me with a dread look. 'I have seen it, Miss Butterworth. I have faced enemy combatants on three continents but never encountered anything I could not explain. I hesitate to call it a dragon, but it flies and breathes fire and has wings. Whatever it is, if it comes back, I intend to catch it or kill it.'

'By shooting it?' questioned DI Munroe. 'Your men tried that already.'

'It was dark, and they were shooting at a fast-moving black target. They missed. That is all.'

The detective wasn't ready to let her point go. 'That is not what their reports claim. They stated that their bullets hit it but had no effect.'

Captain Duncan's features hardened. 'They are mistaken. You can investigate all you want, Cassie. If it invades the palace grounds again, it is my problem to deal with, not yours.'

DI Munroe was becoming visibly annoyed. 'Firing shots inside the palace grounds is just as dangerous as …'

'As what?' he cut her off. 'As letting a fire breathing creature stalk the palace and burn people to death? It has killed twice already, Detective Inspector.'

While they were arguing, I was gathering my thoughts. I was here and this was supposed to be my area of expertise. Whatever had come into the palace grounds and however it had arrived here, my experience assured me that it was not something paranormal.

Interrupting their increasingly heated discussion, I coughed loudly and started speaking. 'Okay, I want to start by stating that what we are dealing with is a man in a suit.' Neither Munroe nor Duncan saw need to hide their surprise. 'It always is,' I insisted before either could argue. 'The firm I work for specialises in dealing with cases like this and there is never a paranormal explanation. The suit might be high-tech, but it is still a suit.'

'That can fly?' questioned Captain Duncan.

'And spit fire and is bulletproof,' I added. 'Still a suit. My first question is to do with why it is here. Why the palace? This place has an armed squad of soldiers so even if the suit is made of a material that deflects bullets, coming here is an incredible risk. The 'man' must be after something. What do you have of value in the palace?'

Munroe and Duncan both snorted laughs.

'Of value?' questioned Munroe. 'Even the toilet paper is worth a fortune.'

Captain Duncan agreed. 'There are priceless paintings, ornaments, and objects everywhere. Then there is the desire to break into the palace just for bragging rights. For many, just getting to take a selfie inside the palace is enough motive to break in.'

'Hence the palace-assigned senior detective,' pointed out DI Munroe.

I sniffed in a deep breath as I absorbed what should have been obvious to me.

Captain Duncan prompted me to speak. 'Any idea as to what we might be dealing with or how we can stop it?' His tone was mocking.

With both the detective and the senior soldier watching me, I shuffled my feet and gave some thought before speaking. I didn't want to appear flustered or without the ability to provide a clear answer, but that was how I managed to come across.

Before I could answer him, Captain Duncan cut me off. 'Right, good plan. I suspect I could have come up with that by myself.' His response to me taking some time to think was both rude and unnecessary.

'I doubt that attitude will help,' I snapped. 'I arrived a few minutes ago. Do you think perhaps I might be permitted enough time to absorb the information I am presented with?'

The solider snorted a bored laugh. 'Time? Civilians always want time so they can avoid making a decision. We have a *man*, if I accept your belief, in a suit. All I need to do is create an ambush, lure him into my kill box, and end this. We can pick over the why and who of it once he is disabled or dead. If I ignore your looney theory, I then have a creature I cannot explain but it will die just the same when my troops cut it to shreds.'

'You plan to kill him,' I scoffed. 'How is that working out for you so far? Didn't I hear that your bullets have no effect on it? What do you propose to use next? Artillery?'

The captain's features contorted in rage, unhappy to be spoken down to by a young woman, but when he spoke, he wasn't addressing me.

'There is no need for this … woman to be here, Cassandra. I shall keep this foolishness from my report, but you had better get rid of her now.'

I thought DI Munroe was going to agree with him and that my trip would prove to be wasted, but she rounded on the soldier, glaring up at him.

'You don't tell me what to do, Raef. I'm the palace detective, you're the guard dog.'

Captain Duncan reacted as if slapped, reeling away from the imagined blow only to then bare his teeth. He was about to retort when DI Munroe stopped him.

'I will arrest you if you threaten me,' she stated calmly.

Seething, but holding his tongue, Captain Duncan held back whatever it was he wanted to say. When a couple of seconds had passed and his anger was wrestled under control, he twitched his eyes to me and then back to the police detective.

'My men will bring the creature down. Then we will find out if it is a man or not.' Spinning on his heel, he left no opportunity for argument as he stormed from the room.

'Raef, wait!' DI Munroe called after him. 'Raef, we need to work together.'

His footsteps echoed in the hall outside as he continued unabated. When they faded into the distance, DI Munroe swore.

We were going to get down to business in a second, but before we did there was something I wanted to clear up. I had seen the looks passing between the two of them.

'Did I notice some tension between the two of you?' I asked casually. DI Munroe's eyes had been cast down, but she snapped them up to meet mine now.

'It's that obvious, huh?' She swore under her breath again. 'We dated briefly. I guess I liked the alpha male thing, at least, I did until I got to know him a little better. He's a bully, one of those men who thinks they know what is best for the woman in their life and is prepared to tell them how to behave and … well, you get the picture. We only slept together once. It has been a problem working with him ever since.'

Now that I had a clear picture and could better understand why he went from reasonable to ridiculous so quickly, I could focus on what needed to be done.

I didn't have a lot to go on and the dragon hadn't been seen for three days. Would it ever return? Was there still a danger to the people in the palace or was there ever? Two people had died but was one of them the intended target or were they both unfortunate victims?

There were a lot more questions than answers and it was time to start picking the detective's brain. I didn't get to do that though because Cassie got a phone call.

A Royal Arrival. Thursday, October 12th 2001hrs

I could only hear one half of her conversation, and pretended I wasn't listening as I busied myself going over the meagre evidence.

What was instantly clear from what I did overhear was the arrival of someone unexpected.

When she abruptly ended the call, she tapped me on my shoulder.

'I can't leave you in here or free to roam the palace. Sorry, I need to go so you'll just have to come with me.'

I hooked my handbag with my left hand, scooping it up and onto my shoulder as I went out the door she held open as an unspoken invitation to leave.

Then I followed her, weaving through the corridors in the bowels of the palace. With time to absorb what I had learned and give some thought to how I might tackle the case with a view to resolving the mystery, the first inkling of a plan tickled away deep in my brain.

However, I was feeling quite discombobulated. It was hard to concentrate on anything because I was in Buckingham Palace.

Actual Buckingham Palace!

Had I known this was how my day was going to turn out, I would have chosen better clothes this morning. Everything I looked at and everywhere I looked, the décor and furnishings were incredible. The paintings on the walls, the walls themselves even and the way the corners at each doorway were carved and infilled with gold leaf would look ridiculous anywhere else, but here it just made the place look like a palace.

My eyes were out on stalks constantly.

It made me wish I was wearing a ballgown or a really sharp business suit. Instead, I had gone with skinny white jeans, caramel leather ankle boots with a low, chunky heel, a thick knitted sweater over a silk vest and a leather jacket that matched my boots. I felt very much underdressed.

'Lord Chamberlain,' DI Munroe called as we came into a large hall.

My belly did a little flip flop when a man turned to look our way. Was I supposed to bow or something?

The man was just taking off his coat. There was moisture on it to let us know it was raining outside. I wondered how long it might last.

Lord Chamberlain was short and a little scruffy. I judged his age to be early thirties though he looked older due to a receding hairline which made his skull look like it had forced its way through his hair to emerge on top. His chin was weak, he didn't stand straight, and his eyes were watery.

There were two men in palace livery behind him and half a dozen large cases piled two high – his luggage I guessed. I couldn't fill that many cases if I packed everything I owned.

'Ah, Detective Inspector. Lovely to see you. How are things at the palace?'

She didn't bow when she reached him, so I didn't either, falling in behind and to her left where I remained silent and hoped I wouldn't be noticed.

'Were you expected, Lord Chamberlain?' she asked. 'I was not informed.'

'Why would you be informed?' boomed a deep voice from our left. Another man was coming down a short flight of steps to join us and he bore a stern expression. In his late sixties or maybe slightly older, he wore a fine tweed suit and waistcoat with a chain for a pocket watch. His tie … I couldn't be certain, but I was willing to bet it was from a military regiment.

'Sir Cuthbert!' exclaimed Lord Chamberlain in the same manner one might when seeing a favourite relative.

DI Munroe leaned her head across to whisper, 'Lord Cuthbert is the head of the palace staff.'

Sir Cuthbert came to a stop a few feet away, addressing the royal family member warmly before turning his attention to Cassie.

'Should you not be engaged in your investigation, Detective Inspector?' he posed the question in a rhetorical manner. 'Perhaps I should speak with the commissioner and see if he can motivate you to do your job.' There was a story there and I was beginning to feel that I needed to know what it was even if she did not wish to share it with me.

With a calm voice, though I could feel the tension radiating off, her DI Munroe replied.

'Sir Cuthbert, I am doing my job, but it is made far more complex when I do not know who is staying in the palace.'

'This is not a planned visit,' Lord Chamberlain interjected with a smile. 'My brother, Eddie, sent for me. I've no idea what it might be about. Probably something to do with papa.'

If I had it right, I was looking at the elder Lord Chamberlain. DI Munroe named the only royal in residence as Edward and said that he was the younger of two sons of the Duke of Westborough.

Whether I was right about the relationship between the two brothers was something I was going to have to ask about later because Lord Chamberlain's gaze was firmly locked on me.

'And who is this fine young filly?' he guffawed lecherously. 'A newcomer to the palace. Perhaps I should show you around my family's humble abode, eh? I bet you and I could find a way to while away the evening.'

My jaw dropped open, baffled by what the correct response in such a situation might be. He was hitting on me in front of DI Munroe and Sir Cuthbert and openly propositioning me with ... what? Sex? That was how it sounded.

'This is Jane Butterworth, sir.' DI Munroe introduced me. 'She is here to deal with the *incident* we had last week.'

'Yes, yes. I heard about that. Some kind of break in and a fire, Eddie said. Terrible business.'

'You will be staying the night?' DI Munroe enquired.

Lord Chamberlain shot her a cheeky smile. 'Saucy.'

Munroe sighed and rolled her eyes. I was coming to understand that his flirting was automatic and continuous just as much as it was unwelcome and pointless. Even if he was gay and I was single, I would rather chew my arm off than spend time in the loathsome man's company.

Sir Cuthbert's gaze was fixed firmly on Cassie and me, his unspoken instruction quite clear – go away.

'If you will excuse us, Lord Chamberlain,' DI Munroe ignored Sir Cuthbert and spoke only to the royal family member. 'We have duties to which we must attend.' DI Munroe backed up, bumping against my arm as a signal to turn around and go the other way.

I did just that, but in so doing also took my eyes off the member of the peerage – the first I had ever met – and thus lowered my guard.

'Aaah!' I cried in surprise when he pinched my bottom. Caught out by his unexpected move, I forgot to use my *Jane* voice and now everyone was looking at me.

Blushing, and making sure to employ the correct voice, I snapped, 'Keep your hands to yourself.'

DI Munroe, still frowning and uncertain what she should make of the deeper voice she just heard, nevertheless agreed with me.

'Yes, sir. That was sexual assault, sir. Be warned.'

He didn't like being told off but raised his hands in surrender as we walked away.

I expected the police detective to ask outright if I was a girl or a boy when we got around the corner, but the subject she went with was the presence of the additional royal.

'I don't like it,' she revealed quietly. 'I don't like that his brother refused to leave, but now he is inviting family members here to join him?'

We had ascended to ground level to intercept Lord Chamberlain because DI Munroe wanted to know why he had chosen to visit. Heading back to her office, we were about to descend a staircase when shadows shot by outside and we both heard shouting.

A Crazy Plan. Thursday, October 12th 2012hrs

In the space of a heartbeat, we were running. I had to follow the detective – the palace is a maze, and I might never have found a door without her to guide me.

I was shocked to see her produce a weapon. It came from somewhere inside her jacket, a small handgun – what type I could not tell you – but it fit snugly into her tiny hand as she held it down to her right side and ran for the door.

We burst into the garden at the back of Buckingham Palace where a huge lawn stretched out towards tall trees. Moonlight, peeking between clouds, reflected off a distant lake. The rain had stopped, just about, but the fresh scent one always gets after the rain lingered.

My heart was banging in my chest, adrenalin pumping through my veins as I skidded to a stop on the wet flagstones outside.

Half a second was all it took to assess what we were seeing. The soldiers were running through some drills.

There was no danger, that was the first thing to take away. The uniformed men, wearing combat fatigues rather than the impressive red tunics with the bearskin hats, were dashing here and there, but doing so in a controlled, not panicked or urgent manner.

DI Munroe muttered something I couldn't catch, her words not intended for anyone to hear probably, and she turned around to go back inside.

'This dragon case has given me the jitters,' she complained. 'Raef regularly has them performing exercises. Until recently, I think they all considered it a waste of time – the palace was never going to be attacked.

I guess now his soldiers must accept he was right to ensure they were ready. At least with them outside, if the dragon comes back, they will be able to repel it.'

'Yeah, about that,' I started, letting the teasing sentence get her attention. 'Maybe we shouldn't go all out to scare it away when it comes back.'

DI Munroe offered me an expression that questioned my sanity.

'What are you proposing? We leave the door open and invite it inside?'

'Shooting it out of the sky is fraught with danger because the bullets will fall to earth in a populated area,' I reminded her. 'Plus, it seems impervious to the injuries inflicted. If you cannot shoot it down, perhaps we should be looking at alternative ways to stop it.'

'Such as?' she encouraged me to expand.

I drew in a deep breath and laid out my idea. When I finished, Cassie – she got bored with me calling her detective inspector the whole time and invited the use of her first name – took her time responding.

When she did, I could see she was trying to find the right words. 'That is probably the craziest plan I have ever heard.' I was going to have to convince her. 'But,' she held up a hand to stop me talking, 'it could actually work. It's not as if I have a better plan myself.'

There were a few problems with cases like this one. A crime occurred that defied explanation, but we like those at Blue Moon because it is where we come in. Tempest taught me to look at things differently from how others might and by doing so we solve most of the cases we get.

It takes a while though. If there is no continued threat, that is not too much of a problem, but the flying, bulletproof, fire-spitting apparition at the centre of this case could return at any time.

It raised the stakes and I wanted to set a trap to catch it. However, we could not calculate how long it would be before it returned. It could be in five days or five minutes so my daft idea might bear fruit, but there was no telling when.

To that end we would set it up, but then Cassie was going to have to employ people to monitor it.

Since she was in agreement, I posed the next obvious question. 'So, where do we get a net?'

The Younger Brother. Thursday, October 12th 2026hrs

The answer was closer than I expected. The soldiers had an indoor five-a-side court with goals at each end. Cassie was convinced we were more likely to run into trouble from the soldiers when they found out than we were from the dragon if it returned.

Watching for the guardsmen, we snuck across the palace grounds to get to their recreation area. My plan, daft as it sounds, was to leave a window open and invite the dragon into the palace. Cassie didn't want it inside, but under pressure to find out who was behind it, and willing to admit she had no faith in the soldiers' ability to catch it or shoot it down, she was willing to try anything.

It would all be arbitrary if the dragon didn't come back.

Cassie led a winding route to get to where she wanted to go – avoiding the soldiers she explained. They were easy to avoid because they never set foot inside the residential areas of the palace. She didn't, as a rule, but was free to go where she needed within reason.

Explaining as she went, I learned most of the soldiers who chased the dragon three nights ago had entered the palace proper for the first time. They didn't live within the grounds but came in for their rotation of guard duty, typically lasting twenty-four hours, then went home or back to their barracks again. The ceremonial duty – the very public guardsmen photographed by thousands of tourists a day – was considered an honour, but not one that required them to enter the palace.

They had a guard house at the back of the grounds where it was tucked away from visitors' eyes and a small recreational area so they could exercise in their downtime. If they fancied a kick about tonight, they were going to discover their goal nets had been requisitioned.

The nets proved unwieldy and cumbersome. Even balled up carefully so we could carry them, they were heavier than I had anticipated, and bits kept slipping from my hands to snag my feet which I couldn't see with my arms full.

Grunting and panting, I stopped on a landing for Cassie to catch up and tell me which way I now needed to go.

'Hello,' said a voice from behind me.

I turned to find a man eyeing me curiously. He wore slouchy grey cotton jogging bottoms and had bare feet. His top half was covered by a faded Hackett polo shirt. Cradled under his left arm, a small brown sausage dog slept with his head on his owner's forearm. The man had a mug of steaming tea in his right hand, the string of the teabag looped around the mug's handle.

He was in his late twenties, making him a few years older than me, but goodness he was handsome. I took in his features and proportions, observing the small stain on his shirt where food had dropped, and the marks on his thumbs where his uncalloused hands had been rubbed raw.

You've got a boyfriend. The words echoed in my head, reminding me that I wasn't supposed to be dribbling at the man-candy somehow making grubby casual wear look good. The thin waist and wide shoulders were complemented by a strong jaw and dazzling blue eyes.

Eyeing me critically, he took a sip from his mug before saying. 'I do not recall seeing you before. I would shake your hand, but you appear to have them both full. I'm Eddie.'

I gulped, trying to find my voice as I shuffled the net to get a hand free.

'I'm Jane,' I squeaked, losing control of the stupid net, and dropping it. The net didn't want to be dropped though, opting as a sign of its displeasure to snag the handbag I'd looped around my neck to keep my hands free.

It pulled my head down, causing Eddie to dart forward and rescue me.

'Here, let me take that,' he offered, scooping the goal net effortlessly while handing me his mug to hold. 'Where are we going with it, Jane?' he smiled in a way that made my tummy tighten.

'The western terrace,' puffed Cassie, finally broaching the top step to arrive on the landing too. Seeing then who had asked the question, she inclined her head. 'Lord Chamberlain.'

'Detective Inspector Munroe, good evening. Might I enquire as to what you ladies are up to? It seems you have a devilish plan afoot.'

Cassie blew him off with a casual dismissal. 'Nothing exciting, I can assure you, sir.'

He wasn't fooled. 'Really? It looks to me like you are planning to net our fiery friend if he makes another appearance.'

Switching topics, quite deliberately I felt sure, Cassie asked him, 'Did your brother find you, sir?'

Lord Edward Chamberlain's features froze, just for a second. 'Find me?'

'Yes, sir,' replied Cassie. 'He arrived half an hour ago. He claimed you invited him, sir.'

'I hardly think so,' replied Lord Chamberlain with a scoffing tone. 'Nugent has no time for his little brother. He hasn't had a civil word for me in years.'

'Why is that?' I asked without thinking, my cheeks colouring when the royal swung his gorgeous gaze my way. Was it too late to add a 'sir' now?

If I had just insulted him by addressing him as if we were equals, the member of the peerage didn't seem to notice.

'Father favoured me,' Edward revealed. 'He always did since I was born. Ever since I came along and stole father's attention away from a young boy, my elder brother has hated me for it. I doubt it helps that my brother …' he struggled to complete the rest of the sentence and I wondered what he might have been about to say when he added, 'Well, I don't think Nugent is happy that he lost his hair so young and mine appears to be going nowhere.'

Edward had been looking for a way to modestly point out how vastly different the brothers were. Coming from the same genetic soup, they could not be more different. Where the elder brother and heir to the Dukedom (is that the right term?) had a weak chin, poor posture, and no hair, his brother looked like an Italian aftershave model.

'He's in the palace, is he?' Lord Chamberlain sought to confirm.

'Indeed, sir,' replied Cassie. 'Perhaps he is looking for you.'

I was curious to learn why the elder lord might visit if his younger brother had not invited him. If they got along so badly, why visit at all? It was all a little bizarre and was making my Spidey senses tingle.

'I shall look for him once I have helped you ladies get to where it is you are going.'

'No need, sir,' argued Cassie. 'We can manage.'

'No doubt,' he agreed with a smile. 'But I am nothing but a lazy royal with too little to occupy my time. Some exercise will do me good.' He plopped his dog on the carpet. 'You can get some exercise too, Henkel.' While his dog stretched and arched his back, Lord Edward scooped my net under one arm, and Cassie's under the other, before suggesting she should, 'Lead on.'

In a bedroom at the back of the palace where it overlooked the garden and the lake beyond, Cassie opened a window to let in the cold night air.

'The trap will be here?' asked Lord Chamberlain, nodding his head as if he could envisage the dragon becoming ensnared.

'Perhaps, sir,' Cassie was attempting to shoo the royal member away. 'Thank you for your help. Miss Butterworth and I will take it from here.'

'But I can help,' he protested. I couldn't tell, but wondered if he was bored and in need of something to do or trying to find a legitimate reason not to find his brother.

'Police business, sir,' argued the detective inspector.

Lord Chamberlain or Eddie, as I had come to mentally label him, backed away with his hands up and a broad smile showing off his perfect teeth.

'Yes, quite right, I'm sure. Don't want the inbred royal mucking things up.' He shot me a smile and a wink. Eddie, fourteenth in line for the crown was self-deprecating and modest. That he was willing to make jokes about himself and act the fool made me feel yet more drawn to him.

He backed away to the door, made a show of bowing before he left the room and vacated it with a final wish for good luck and good hunting.

I watched the empty space in the doorway for a few more seconds before turning my attention back to the task at hand.

The nets were bundled on the carpet in two piles. Somehow we two girls had to erect them in such a way that they would ensnare the dragon if it came into the room.

A cold breeze blew through the open window making me wish I had picked a thicker coat. Cassie felt it too and it gave urgency to our movements, both to keep us warm and to get the job done so we could go somewhere that was less breezy.

I closed the bedroom door and picked up one of the nets. This was my daft idea – I needed to be the one to present a solution.

Outside in the dark we could hear Raef's soldiers dashing to-and-fro. I didn't want to think of them as trigger-happy fools, but their guns scared me. Shooting at the dragon achieved nothing in their previous attempts. What did Captain Duncan think they would gain from repeating the same thing?

If they were shooting at it, I wanted to be nowhere near them.

Reusing the ornate cord intended to tie the curtains back, the windows themselves, once opened inwards, plus a great deal of puffing, panting, and the use of rude words, we got one of the nets erected. It hung in such a manner that should the dragon come through the window, it would hit the net and be instantly ensnared.

That was the idea. How well it might work and what we did then was anyone's guess. Standing back, Cassie admitted she was impressed.

'It's better than anything I might have come up with,' she conceded. 'Let's put the other one up in a different room.'

We did precisely that, grunting, straining, and balancing on chairs to reach high enough, but ten more minutes of work gave us a second trap.

Taking my hand for balance as she stepped down to the floor, Cassie remarked, 'I guess all we can do now is wait.'

I nodded. 'Let's not wait here though. It's cold.' My fingers were going numb from the cool air spilling through the open window.

'Tea?' suggested the detective. She was rubbing her hands together and blowing on them, the air in front of her face a billowing cloud as her breath hit the cold.

But here's the thing about setting a trap – you need to then watch it. Only once we left the cold and drafty bedroom on a mission to get mugs of hot tea did it occur to me that should the dragon make an appearance we had no way of knowing about it.

'Oh, bother,' I commented when Cassie pointed out my thoroughly obvious mistake. By then we were halfway back to her office in the bowels of the palace. 'I need to go back.'

'I'll go,' Cassie volunteered. 'You get the teas.'

I was about to suggest we trade jobs because I wasn't sure I could find my way to her office by myself and certain I would never find my way back to the bedrooms with the traps in. It was probably easy once a person became better acquainted with the palace, but to me it all looked the same. None of that left my mouth though, because the air filled with the sound of gunfire.

Fire. Thursday, October 12th 2048hrs

When the shooting started, there was a heartbeat of indecision where we both looked at each other, and then, without either one of us saying anything, we were running.

If the dragon was here – I couldn't imagine what else the troops were firing at – it meant right now was our best hope for the trap to work. Would it see the open windows? We left table lamps on, rather than each bedroom's main lights. They cast enough light to show the easy access point but not so much that the presence of the nets would be obvious.

Or so we hoped.

Racing up a flight of stairs to get back to the next floor, my pulse was through the ceiling. I had to tell myself that whatever we were dealing with, it was not a mythical or supernatural creature. It wasn't a demon or a fire-breathing dragon or anything else, even if the eyewitness reports suggested otherwise.

As further proof that I hadn't really thought through my plan, it dawned on me that if we burst through the bedroom doors and found the dragon trapped by our net, it would probably still be able to breathe fire. Not only did we have nothing with which to subdue it, we had no protection against the flames. Even St George thought to take a shield with him!

No sooner had my latest worry registered in my brain than DI Munroe reminded me that she was armed. She yanked her gun from its holster as we got to the bedroom door and shoulder-barged into the room with the weapon pointing at the window.

I ran in after her giving little thought to my own safety. I wanted to see if we had been successful.

The net, however, was still in place.

Cassie yelled, 'The other room!' and spun about to go back out. I blocked her path and needed to get my own body facing the other way. Before I could, I saw the look in her eyes.

It was raw terror.

She wasn't looking at me. Her eyes were aimed above my head to where the ceiling met the wall and twisting around to follow her horrified gaze, I found out what had her so scared.

Hovering in the air just above the door we needed to escape through was a black apparition. Hidden in the shadows, but easy to see nevertheless because its bright orange eyes were glaring down at us, the dragon slowly beat its wings.

Its wingspan was as wide as the body and legs were long. Even though the room was lit, the small table lamps cast shadows and it was hard to make out fine detail. The one thing that registered in my terrified mind was that its proportions were that of a human.

My brain felt disconnected from the rest of me. I could not explain what I was looking at, but it was flying, and it had us trapped. My knees wanted to fold out from underneath me and I questioned whether there would be anything left of my remains other than a sooty mess.

A second ticked by, no one moving until I felt Cassie grabbing hold of my shoulder. She was shouting something, but my eyes were locked on the dragon's featureless face. The orange eyes made it hard to see any other part of the dragon so all I had was an impression of wingspan and the black scales covering its body.

Until the flame appeared.

At the same time, from the corner of my eye I spotted Cassie's gun rising. Her grip on my shoulder was tugging me backward and what she had shouted a second ago finally sunk into my head.

'Window!'

Her gun went off, a thunderous boom that was so close to my face it seemed to shake the fillings in my teeth. I was twisting, trying to keep my balance as she yanked at my clothing. The open window was right there. It didn't offer much as a means of escape and the fall to the ground had to be at least fifty feet.

We might not survive hitting the ground, but the expanding flame behind me as the dragon started to spew fire left me no choice but to find out.

The gun went off again. I hadn't seen either shot land but since the dragon wasn't down or showing signs of wanting to give up, whether Cassie hit it or not mattered little.

We ducked under the bottom edge of the net roughly four feet off the ground and as I felt the wall of heat making the air behind me blister, the pair of us dove through the hole in the wall and into the night beyond.

Flame shot over our heads searing my lungs with its heat. The light accompanying it was so bright I lost my vision. Was that a mercy? I wouldn't see the ground coming at me. I would just hit it and that would be that. Much better than getting cooked extra crispy.

How long would it take to fall fifty feet? The answer, it turned out before my eyesight returned, was far shorter than I could have imagined.

The air whooshed from my lungs as I slammed into gravel with my chest. It hurt, but rolling to a stop with my senses reeling, I knew I had something wrong.

'Come on!' screamed Cassie, firing her gun again. Her hand found my arm, gripping the flesh around my bicep so hard it must have bruised as she pulled me to get up.

The bright light in my eyes was fading, leaving a corona behind, but I could see now that the ground we hit was less than four feet beneath the level of the window.

There was a balcony or parapet running along outside! The correct term for it mattered not one jot. The point is, I hadn't seen it in the dark earlier. Too focused on erecting the net, and deliberately not looking down as I balanced near the window, I just didn't spot that it was there.

Getting dragged along by Cassie, I stumbled and almost fell. She was getting away from the window. The curtains inside were ablaze, so too the net from the football goal which was now the thing stopping the dragon from following us.

I saw its black shape illuminated by the dancing flames as I ran beside Cassie. She had a radio in her hand, but the message she needed to pass was already out there – the palace is on fire, and the dragon is inside.

We stopped running, facing back the way we came when we reached the extent of the balcony. We were two or more rooms along from the one now filled with fire and gasping for breath.

Neither one of us said anything until Raef's voice screeched over the airwaves.

'What did you do? You let it in, you idiot!'

DI Munroe swore loudly and lifted the radio back to her mouth.

'Send your QRF to the west wing, Captain Duncan. They have a fire to fight. There is an intruder in the palace, evacuate everyone to the basement level. I will find the Lords Chamberlain.'

'You'll do nothing!' snapped Captain Duncan. 'I am in command here. You have done enough. Return to your quarters and stay out of our way. Out.'

The radio clicked off, Captain Duncan ending his conversation with the detective in a manner that left little room for argument.

Cassie swore again.

'Is that right?' I asked, still trying to get my breath back. My chest hurt where I slammed it into the gravel, and I felt certain I was going to need a few Band-Aids to deal with the cuts and grazes. My clothes were ruined too, changing my stance on wishing I had worn my best outfit, but I was upright and able to function. 'Is he in charge?'

'Yes,' Cassie spat between tight lips. 'There is an intruder in the palace and threat to life. This is all his jurisdiction.'

'What does that mean for you?' I managed to ask between laboured breaths. 'Are you in trouble?'

'I don't care,' she growled, her words aimed at herself more than me I thought. 'I need to get inside and make sure that ... *thing* doesn't hurt anyone. God, I am such an idiot! I practically invited it inside.'

Without another word, she lined up her gun and fired into the nearest window. I was about to ask what the heck she was doing, but the answer was obvious; she had shot out the locking mechanism on the inside and was now forcing the window open.

The net and the open windows had been my idea. I knew that would matter little when they came to account for what had happened. Detective Inspector Munroe invited me here, so everything thereafter was on her. I parked the guilt I felt building in my gut and climbed through the open window after her.

A stampede of footsteps heralded soldiers arriving in the hallway outside. When we emerged from the bedroom, half a dozen twitchy guns swung our way. It was enough to make me cry out in alarm.

There were thirty or more of the quick-reaction force filling the hallway. Some had their guns pointing this way and that, their non-commissioned officers shouting orders. Others had their rifles slung across their backs as they carried firehoses.

They were tackling the fire and their swift reactions would wrestle it under control before it could spread from the room in which it started, but the door to that room was open and the dragon was somewhere else now.

Amid the deafening noise of high-pressure water dousing the flames and the continued shouting of soldiers giving orders, the sound of Captain Duncan's voice still reached my ears.

'I told you to leave the area!' he shouted, weaving through the men filling the corridor.

Sir Cuthbert appeared, halting Raef's progress with a hand. I had to move position to see where he had come from, spotting a set of stairs I had not noticed before. They were narrow and lacking the sweeping architectural notes I saw everywhere else.

'Sir Cuthbert again,' swore Cassie.

'What's his role here?' I asked. It hadn't been pertinent before, but he was getting involved now.

Cassie spat, 'He's an officious interfering old busybody. However, his official title is Master of the Palace. His word is law here.'

'Captain Duncan, kindly explain yourself,' Sir Cuthbert demanded. 'What on earth is happening here? I heard Detective Inspector Munroe claim there is an intruder in the palace!'

'That's right,' snarled the captain, his eyes not on the man in the suit, but aimed firmly at Cassie. 'She let him in,' he pointed an accusing hand in our direction. 'The woman with her, if that is what she is,' he added snidely, 'is some daft paranormal investigator. Unable to solve this case herself, Detective Inspector Munroe is clutching at straws and willing to turn to any charlatan trickster who claims to be able to help.'

'A paranormal investigator?' the master of the palace repeated disbelievingly, his tone dripping with derision and horror as he turned to see where the senior soldier's hand pointed. 'What the devil ...'

'Exactly, Sir Cuthbert, exactly. She's completely lost the plot, and this fire is the result. Rest assured my men have it under control. It will not spread. We are sweeping the upper galleries now, attempting to find the intruder.'

Both men were glaring at me and Cassie with utter contempt. I had a dozen responses lined up but couldn't tell if speaking my mind would make things better or worse for the detective.

I never got to find out, because a shout rang out.

'It's on the roof!'

Fire at Will. Thursday, October 12th 2055hrs

The cry came from inside the torched bedroom. One of the soldiers checking the blaze was properly out – the fire brigade would be along soon to check their handiwork, I felt certain – had seen something through the open window.

His colleagues, dropping their fire-fighting equipment, were running to his side to get a look too.

I was about to follow, my right foot just starting to lift from the carpet when I heard a terrible cry of alarm.

'Help me! Someone help me! There's a dragon!' The voice was unmistakably that of Lord Edward Chamberlain, the handsome youngest son of a duke.

I was not the only one who heard it.

Cassie and Captain Duncan banged into each other as they both rushed to get into the destroyed bedroom. Water dripped from every surface, and the carpet squelched beneath my feet as I raced to get a look for myself.

Taller than Cassie, and indeed many of the soldiers with my heels to add a few inches, I could see over their heads. All eyes were trained on the rooftop adjacent to us and two stories above.

Where the rear façade of the palace was anything but a flat face, the portion we were looking at jutted out into the rear gardens. High up on the parapet, Eddie ran for his life. I could see something in his hands, his little dog, Henkel, no doubt.

Holding the dog as he ran was slowing him down, preventing the peer from pumping his arms, and he really needed to go faster because the dragon was coming right for him.

The black shape swooped down over the palace rooftop, coming from high in the night sky and only visible because it created an even blacker spot in the darkness. Until the flame appeared in its mouth again, that is.

'A man in a suit, is it?' screamed Raef, shoving me roughly to one side. He had no further words for me and wasn't hanging around to hear my reply. 'Out the window, all of you!' he commanded his men. 'Two fire teams. Corporal Bates take five men to the south corner and stay out of sight until you hear my shout. We are going to drive it to you! When I give the command, unleash hell!'

The soldiers scrambled to get out of the window, hastily obeying Raef's orders. Shunted aside and ignored, I could hear them making their weapons ready.

'Fire!' bellowed Captain Duncan, his order resulting in a deafening cacophony of shots as the soldiers attempted to shoot the black apparition from the air.

I couldn't hope to estimate how many shots were fired by the dozen or more soldiers to Raef's left and right, but more than a hundred easily.

Cassie was screaming something, her voice hopelessly drowned out by the gunfire.

Eddie vanished around the side of the roof, running for all he was worth just as a gout of flame shot from the dragon's mouth. It lit the night sky. Like a lance of bright light, it beat the darkness into submission and burned my eyesight for a half second.

In that moment of bright illumination, I saw bullets strike the dark form of the dragon all along its flank. The guardsmen were accurate, but the wounds they inflicted made no difference to the creature.

The flame and its searing brightness were gone no sooner than they appeared but having looked at it, any hope of picking out the dragon against the dark sky was gone.

The soldiers were still shooting at the spot where it had been and perhaps it was still there though I couldn't see it at all.

Cassie slammed into Captain Duncan, knocking his trigger finger away and sending him sprawling into the soldiers to his left.

'Cease fire, you idiot!' she screamed into his face. 'Where are those bullets landing? You've no idea, man! Fire another shot and I'll arrest you myself!'

Her actions had the desired effect, the shooting petered out in the next second as the soldiers turned their attention to their commander.

Grunting and growling in his anger and disbelief, Raef pushed himself off the ground. I thought he might attempt to strike the detective, but what he did was much worse. He pointed his rifle directly at her face.

'Get in the way again, Munroe, and I will have you bound and gagged. This is your mess, and I am going to fix it. Protecting the royal family and the palace is my job.'

'You almost shot Lord Edward,' Cassie spat, paying no attention to the muzzle of the gun hovering a foot in front of her eyes. 'Your shots are having no impact on the dragon, and you are endangering life. When this is over, I will arrest you for threatening me. Are we clear on that?' She was speaking through gritted teeth, rage bubbling beneath the surface, but being kept in check by an iron will.

A voice from behind her said, 'Captain Duncan is in command here, Detective Inspector Munroe.' I turned to find the Master of the Palace, Sir Cuthbert, coming to Raef's side. Ignoring Cassie, he spoke over her head. 'Carry on, Captain Duncan. Take down that beast at all costs.'

I could see Cassie fuming. She was the sole voice of reason – no one was going to pay any attention to me – and she had no ability to influence events.

'Where did it go?' demanded Captain Duncan, turning back to his troops. 'Can anyone see the target?' His words were urgent yet controlled – he wasn't panicking and even if he felt fear, he was doing a great job of hiding it. If anything, I believed he was revelling in the action and drama.

No one could spot where the dragon might have gone, but to me that just meant it was still chasing Eddie and they were both out of sight on the other side of the roof.

Outside, on the gravel covering the parapet, the soldiers were taking off across the palace. They wanted to have a clear shot if the dragon reappeared, and they were running to get to where they last saw it. That would require climbing two floors, but the sound of their boots was already fading, only their officer's loud commands echoing in the night air remained to tell us where they were.

Cassie grabbed my arm, yanking me with her as she ran for the door and the interior of the palace.

'That trigger happy idiot is as likely to kill Lord Edward as save him!'

Sir Cuthbert stepped into her path.

'Detective Inspector Munroe, I believe you should return to your office and wait there. I shall be speaking with your superiors shortly and expect a full report on my desk within the hour. Destruction of palace property is not taken lightly, you know.'

I wondered how the already irate police officer might react to the officious man and got my answer in a spectacular fashion.

'Get out of my way, you old fool!' she placed a stiff hand on his shoulder to push him backward from the room and out in the hallway beyond. 'Do something useful and make sure there are no palace staff in the open. Find everyone you can and get to the basement. Then stay there!'

Much like Captain Duncan had with us, she then dismissed him, uninterested to hear what he might have to say in reply to her instructions.

A volley of shots rang out, the distant sound of men shouting back and forth easy to make out through the thick walls of the palace.

'Where are we going?' I shouted, racing after Cassie as she sprinted down the hallway.

Running as hard as she could, her answer came back as a shout between hard breaths, 'My priority is to keep the family safe! Lord Edward is in trouble, and we must get to him. First, though, I need to check Lord Nugent. He's on the next floor and chances are he's still in his room!'

I was out of breath before we got to the stairs and gasping to get enough air in by the time we had raced up them to the next floor. My lungs were searing but I ran on, chasing after the older, yet fitter police officer and reminded myself, not for the first time, that I needed to visit the gym more regularly.

The palace detective ran like a woman with a mission, ripping along the hallway until she skidded to a halt. She had been going so fast, she almost went past the door she wanted and had to grab hold of the door frame to arrest her forward motion.

Too close on her heels to adjust my trajectory, I collided with her. Mercifully, we stayed upright, Cassie's grip on the doorframe enough to stop me too.

Shaking me off, she slammed the door open, her left shoulder leading as we burst into what I guessed would be Lord Nugent's rooms.

The sight that met our eyes rooted us both to the spot.

Evidence. Thursday, October 12th 2102hrs

Strewn across the carpet were electronic components and pieces of carbon fibre frame like one might find on a high-end bicycle. To my right, I spotted a small barrel. It was silver in colour and bore a warning symbol to tell everyone the contents were highly flammable.

On a couch dead ahead were pieces of black material. I made to move forward, desperately curious to get a closer look but found my way barred by Cassie's arm.

'Touch nothing,' she hissed, her voice quiet as if we might disturb someone.

The obvious conclusion we were both drawing was that Lord Nugent, freshly returned to the palace, was the dragon. Quite how and why was beyond me to fathom yet, but if the creature we saw was a man in a suit, what I could see spread out around the room were the pieces used in its manufacture.

The detective took out her phone and started taking pictures.

We were both breathing heavily and had made enough noise arriving in Lord Nugent's chambers that we could be fairly certain he wasn't here. Nevertheless, Cassie called out to be sure.

'Lord Chamberlain? Lord Nugent, are you here?'

When no answer came back, Cassie set off to check the rest of his suite of rooms.

'Stay here,' she insisted. 'Touch nothing.'

I asked her a question that stopped her before she took another step.

'What did you do to get this post?'

She twisted around to look at me.

'You said it was a punishment,' I reminded her. 'And it's clear Sir Cuthbert believes he holds sway over you. He threatened to call the commissioner earlier.' I knew she didn't want me, or probably anyone, to know her past mistakes, but I was more on the backfoot here than I was used to and I wanted to know the type of person I was working with.

'This is a dangerous environment,' I pointed out when she failed to say anything. 'You saved my life earlier, and I owe you for that, but I want to know who it is that I am trusting with my life.'

Her lip twitched. 'You want to know what I am hiding? How about you go first? What's your real name, Jane?'

I accepted her challenge because she was right. My gender preference made no difference to the matter at hand, but I was hiding something too. I dropped my 'Jane' voice.

'My birth certificate says James,' I admitted. 'I am homosexual and prefer to dress as a woman.'

I got a curt nod from the police detective but no opinion or feedback regarding her thoughts on the matter.

'I started a relationship with my boss,' she revealed with a sigh. 'It went on for several months and I believed he was going to leave his wife to be with me. When she found out, he ended it abruptly. It happened right when he was promoted again and became the commissioner. To get rid of me, on his wife's orders I assume, he sent me here. If you are wondering why I haven't called him out on it and claimed I have been marginalised and unfairly treated, then I guess you don't know how things work in the police. Even if I won such a case, I was knowingly sleeping with a married man and my career would be in the trash either way. I have to make it through my time here, hope he moves on and try to pick my career up afterwards. I did this to myself,' she added as if trying to convince herself it was true.

I resumed speaking in my 'Jane' voice. 'I'm sorry to hear that.' I was at the same time relieved because I had been guessing she was guilty of something far worse than falling for the wrong man.

She gave me a nod of acknowledgement and left me where I was, repeating her instruction to touch nothing.

Left alone, I looked around the room some more. I was way out of my depth and very aware that was how I felt. Usually, I am aware of the need to preserve evidence, but it is not as high on my list as solving the crime and I am always calling the shots. Tonight, I was following the detective inspector around like I was her assistant and beginning to feel quite put out by it.

She left the room, going through a door to the right to explore more of Lord Nugent's chambers and in her absence, I thought about what I had seen so far.

It was a man in a suit. It was Lord Nugent Chamberlain. Eddie said his brother resented him and revealed Lord Nugent lied about being invited to the palace by his younger brother. The elder brother, born without the looks and height of his younger sibling, and without his father's favour, had chosen to remove the thorn in his side. The conjuring of a supernatural creature might seem ridiculous to many, but the Blue Moon Investigation Agency sees this every week.

The police will only investigate for so long before the case finds itself consigned to the unsolved pile. If a death appears to have supernatural causes, you can bet it'll find its way to the cold case file all the sooner.

There was a man behind the murders, and we had the evidence in front of us. Finding it had been easy, and … why was it so easy? The question bonged into my consciousness like a giant bell being rung. Surely, Nugent would have locked his door at the very least? If he wanted to get away with murder, he should have kept all his dragon suit components hidden and never brought them into his private quarters. Why would anyone be so sloppy?

More questions were surfacing, none of which I had answers to.

Yet.

I backed out of the room, making my way into the hallway outside again. I couldn't explain quite what was going through my head at that point, but believing I now knew the identity of the man in the suit, I was going to get his attention and do what the soldiers could not.

I was going to bring the dragon down.

Stalemate. Thursday, October 12th 2117hrs

Jogging rather than sprinting, since I had a stitch in my side and was yet to recover my breathing, I left Cassie in Lord Nugent's chambers and made my way back to the stairs.

I heard her calling my name just before I turned a corner. She had undoubtedly come back into the first room we were in and found me gone. If she came into the hallway looking for me, she would find only empty air as I was already out of sight.

It wasn't a deliberate snub. I chose to leave the detective behind because I recognised my plan to be foolhardy and dangerous and because the plan did not require two persons to place themselves in danger.

As I jogged up the stairs to the top floor of the deserted palace, I kept my footsteps light so Cassie might not know which way I had gone. I could hear her calling for me still, her tone becoming exasperated and annoyed. I could also hear the soldiers outside. There had been no shots fired for several minutes but did that mean the dragon had killed Eddie? Or did it mean it had slipped back inside and they couldn't see it anywhere? Had Lord Nugent flown away having completed his murderous task? There was only one way for me to find out.

On the top floor, I tried doors until I found one that was open. The palace is vast, but I felt assured there would be few rooms that had no windows. I needed to make myself as visible as possible both so the dragon would spot me and so the soldiers would see who it was and not shoot me full of holes.

With the lights on to attract attention on the otherwise dark rear façade of the palace, I left the room again and went to find what I needed.

Thankfully, I didn't have to look far and due to the soldiers' earlier efforts I even had a rough idea where it would be and how to operate it.

Nerves were making my hands shake and I felt sick from the adrenalin coursing through my body. If there was ever a time to rethink my plan and go home to bed instead then this was it. Of course, like a fool, I pressed on.

There was no parapet running around outside the windows at this level. If I fell out of the window, I was going to die when I hit the ground. I kept that thought in my mind as I threw the windows open and climbed up to stand inside the frame.

'Lord Nugent!' I shouted as loudly as my quaking voice would manage. Then I stilled myself and shouted again, even louder. 'LORD NUGENT! I know it's you.'

In the still air of the night outside, not even a faint breeze dared to ruffle my hair. I couldn't see the soldiers – whether this was a deliberate ploy on their part to stay hidden from the dragon so they could ambush it, or simply because the dark absorbed them at this distance, I could not tell.

I had been able to hear them moving and shouting orders, the reports reaching my ears from more than one direction until a moment ago. Now they were silent, undoubtedly staring up at the mad, blonde woman framed in the open window.

What the heck was I doing? The question demanded an answer, but when a dark shadow fell across me, and my pulse tripled its speed, I knew it was too late to change my course of action.

I swept my eyes upward to find the dragon silhouetted against the moon. For the first time, I got a good look at my adversary as it stretched its wings to either side. Unable to fathom what I was seeing earlier, it was obvious now that this was no organic creature. It was staying aloft, but its wings were not beating up and down as they would need to. They moved, but far too slowly to keep it in the air. The wings were for show and, if forced to guess, I would say that it achieved flight because there was a propulsion unit fitted into the suit somewhere. The design was ingenious, the work of a seriously intelligent person to not only conceive but to then realise in the flesh as it were.

Now was not, however, the time to be impressed. It was the time to hold my nerve and pray I wasn't throwing my life away on a hunch.

The soldiers were shouting again, and as the dragon started moving, coming straight for me, they opened fire.

The sudden noise made me jump, my nervous legs twitched, and I almost fell from the window when I lost my footing. With just my left hand, I managed to grasp the top of the window frame to pin myself in place.

If I thought my heart was hammering in my chest before, it had been nothing compared to how it felt now. Biting down against rising bile driven into my throat by fear, I sucked in a deep breath and told myself to be ready.

Unlike the soldiers, whose bullets would fly many hundreds of yards, I needed to let the dragon get close to me if I was going to pull off what they could not.

'Jane! What the ...' Cassie's voice ... her exclamation which was then cut short told me not only that she had found me but had instantly worked out what I was attempting to do.

I could hear her running across the room behind me, but I didn't dare turn to look because the dragon was coming right for me.

I held my breath. Truthfully, I was so scared I forgot to breathe. The effect was the same regardless of which way you look at it, but as I waited, and the voice inside my head screamed at me to run away before I became a fireball, I knew it was already too late to escape.

The dragon zipped through the air, a dark shape discernible only because the night sky was brighter with the lights of the city reflecting off the low clouds.

The bright orange eyes seem to mesmerise me, but when I saw the spark of flame appear in its mouth, I snatched my right hand out from where I hid it behind the curtain, and I yanked back on the lever of the fire hose I held.

The dragon was ten yards away and closing fast. If Lord Nugent saw what I was doing and wanted to swerve, I gave him no chance.

The jet of water hit the dragon just south of its face. I hadn't allowed enough for gravity. Nor had I allowed enough for the force of the water. It drove me backward and I lost my balance. Pitching backward, my arms twitched up just as the lance of fire was beginning to form and I doused it in an instant.

I would have fallen from the window at that point had Cassie not arrived to prop me up. Her assessment of the situation and fast reactions saved me as I was able to hold the improvised water cannon on the dragon.

It should have driven it back or blasted it away. That's what my brain told me. It was hard to see in the dark, but to me it looked as if the water were going right through it and not impacting on the surface.

Screaming in defiance, I held the hose in place, blasting the suit and Lord Nugent. He should have fallen from the sky, but he didn't. The water pressure did succeed in driving the dragon back – it couldn't get any closer to me and each time I saw the fire forming, I hit it again.

Shouts from below – indistinguishable as words – let me know the soldiers were still there and planning something new.

I battled the dragon for twenty seconds or more as it tried to find a way to spew fire at me and I kept pushing it back and dousing the flames. As my arms started to get heavy and my muscles began to cramp from fighting against the backward pressure the jet of water created, I wondered how I was going to overcome the impasse. I couldn't knock Lord Nugent from the sky or make him so heavy from added water that his propulsion unit would no longer keep him airborne, and he couldn't create fire to kill me.

Now that I had tipped my hand and shown I knew who was behind the attacks, he had to kill me and anyone else who might have figured it out. There was a stalemate for now but who was going to tire first?

Me. The answer was going to be me, and I knew it.

A fresh eruption of shooting from below the dragon jolted me. Was I in the line of fire? Were those fools going to hit me instead?

As a fresh reason to be afraid gripped me, I saw the dragon falter. When I first arrived, Cassie told me that the soldiers' bullets had no effect on the creature. I had seen it first-hand for myself a short while ago when it was chasing Eddie. Now I got to see it close up, but though I could offer no explanation for how Lord Nugent's dragon suit made him impervious – the bullets were not bouncing off as they might if striking armour – something had just happened.

I heard the ping of a ricochet, and the dragon dropped a foot. My stream of water passed harmlessly over its head for a moment until I could adjust my angle once more.

Captain Duncan must have seen it too because I picked up his voice over the din of the water. A second later, the rate of fire increased.

Cassie was swearing and screaming blue murder even as she propped me up. All those bullets were going up into the air and they were going to come down somewhere. Somewhere in the middle of London.

So unexpectedly that I almost went forward to chase after it, the dragon disengaged. One moment it had been looking for a way to get to me, the next it was flying away.

I had to drop the hose and cartwheel my arms to stop myself from falling out of the window. Cassie grabbed fistfuls of my clothing, hauling me backward and into the safety of the room. As I caught my breath, she shut off the hose and the sudden drop in noise – the soldiers had stopped shooting too – was startling.

I turned to thank the detective for saving my life, but she wasn't looking at me. Her eyes were going wide as saucers as she gawped out through the open window in the night.

'Look!' she squealed.

It Doesn't Add Up. Thursday, October 12th 2130hrs

The dragon was on fire!

That was what caused Cassie to point and squeal. In the air above the palace, still flying as it headed toward the lake at the far end of the garden, Lord Nugent's flying suit was fast becoming a ball of flame.

Blazing globules of something were leaking from it, falling to the ground below as fizzing fireballs. The dragon flew on and I could no more tear my eyes away from the terrible sight than I could give up drinking tea with my breakfast.

Now easy to see from our elevated position, Cassie and I spotted the soldiers racing after it. Raef was two floors below us on one of the parapets and shouting commands to his troops on the ground. He would follow and they were all to converge and keep firing until it was brought down.

If Cassie was worried about yet more bullets being fired, then she didn't need to be, for the dragon exploded before Raef's troops could start shooting again.

High in the air and visible for miles to anyone looking in the right direction, the fiery shape blossomed into a fireball all its own. Any hope I held that Lord Nugent might land and survive were gone. I wanted to know why he had concocted this insane plan. To build the suit and be able to fly in it was an incredible feat. Surely, it hadn't just been so he could kill his brother because he got the best of his father's genes?

I watched in rapt horror as the dragon fell from the sky.

'Did it fall into the lake?' I questioned, certain I had seen a splash. It confused me because my brain insisted the fireball had just fizzled out in the water, but there were flames visible in the trees on the far side of the lake. A burning spot on the ground showed where the dragon had impacted.

Cassie grabbed at my arm. 'Come on! We have to go!'

Jerked into motion, I ran after her, abandoning the fire hose where it lay.

The same stairs I ascended earlier led all the way back down to the ground floor. I was out of breath yet again, and about to beg that we slow to a walk because it had to be over half a mile to the lake, when Cassie pointed to a golf cart.

There were two parked side by side to our left.

The seats were damp from the earlier rain, but I was mostly soaked from the firehose water and there was no way the police officer was waiting for me to find a tissue with which I could dry my chair.

In fact, I had to hang on for dear life because Cassie had the cart moving almost before I was in it, and it moved faster than I expected. In two seconds, we were shooting across the courtyard and onto the lawn.

Soldiers, weighed down by their heavy kit, were running in the same direction but we caught up to them, passed them, and left them in our wake.

Raef, unseen in the dark, shouted for us to come back for him, but Cassie showed no sign that she had even heard him.

We raced on, Cassie's right foot pressed hard to the floor in the little battery-powered cart. The lake loomed ahead of us, growing larger with each passing second.

There were flames ahead to guide us, easy to spot and in the darkness looking innocent - like a bonfire children could be roasting marshmallows over.

The fire was on the far side of the lake, and the water formed a barrier we had no choice but to go around.

When we finally drew near, the flames were beginning to burn out, which was a mercy because I had worried the trees or bushes nearby might have caught fire too.

Cassie let her foot off the pedal, the cart coasting to a stop some five yards shy of the fire.

I could see the dark lump in the middle of the flames. It wasn't moving but then I'd held no hope that the man inside the suit might still be alive.

Cassie climbed down from her seat, approaching the flaming mess slowly and silently. I half expected her to tell me to stay back, but she didn't.

The flames were dying down, the fuel source depleted, and the suit already burnt away. A yard wide strip around the body was singed, the scrubby grass reduced to smouldering ash but there it stopped and would go no farther.

Voices drew my attention back the way we had come. The soldiers had made good time, running across the open ground to get to us and the majority of them were arriving as a pack. There were a few stragglers behind the main body of men, and somehow Raef was at the front.

'Step away from the body,' he commanded, squeezing the words out between gasps for air.

Detective Inspector Munroe didn't even look his way.

'There is a body on the grounds of the palace, Captain Duncan. That makes this a police matter. Unless you think the body still represents some danger to the royal family?' She cast a questioning look at the tall soldier, daring him to argue.

I wasn't really looking at their exchange though. I was looking at the ground.

There was a footprint. There were several footprints. Where the recent rain had softened the earth, the indentations of a man's oxford shoe were leading back to the palace. I spun around to see where they had come from, but the direction they went was the same one the soldiers were coming from.

Troops rushed by me, scuffing up the dirt and ruining any chance I had to investigate.

Captain Duncan, clearly unhappy with the situation, deferred to Cassie and let her claim her right to control the scene. I was certain she hadn't heard the last of the fire upstairs. It was my fault, but I doubted anyone would care about that.

I hustled to draw her attention to the footprints before they were all gone.

'The royals often come out here walking,' she pointed out in a dismissive manner. 'Any footprints you find could be weeks old.'

'They are not,' I argued. 'The rain this evening would have filled them in. These came after the rain and the edges are crisp.'

She wasn't really listening to me, she had two of the soldiers – they were wearing gloves – attempting to remove the headpiece of the dragon suit. Most of the material on the body was gone, the charred flesh beneath exposed, but the head was formed of something different.

Looking down at it, I observed, 'His body ought to be riddled with bullets.'

Cassie nodded, opting to stay quiet.

'And when I hit him with the fire hose, it should have pushed him away.'

The headpiece came away when one of the soldiers found a clasp under the chin.

'Ma'am?' he asked, checking that they should attempt to slide it off.

The palace detective nodded and the two soldiers, kneeling either side of Lord Nugent's head, carefully eased the black helmet off his head.

His face was burned, but not to the same extent as the rest of his body. It laid to rest any question about who was inside the suit though, for it was Lord Nugent Chamberlain, thirteenth in line to the throne, whose sightless eyes stared up to heaven.

'Sir,' called a voice from the dark, making Captain Duncan lift his chin to see who wanted him.

A cry of anguish caught me by surprise, and I spun around to find Eddie staring at his brother. He was being held back by two of the guardsmen and had Sir Cuthbert at his side. The older man looked weary from the walk across the palace lawn and unable to cope with the gravity of the scene before his eyes.

'Let him through,' commanded Raef.

The handsome younger brother came forward with stumbling steps. Henkel, the little sausage dog, still clasped to his chest. He had escaped his brother on the roof, and I wondered if he had found refuge somewhere or simply evaded the fire when the soldiers drew Nugent's attention with their shots.

There was a whole lot that did not add up, but I wasn't going to get any answers until things had settled down here.

More people were coming from the palace, and looking back across the vast lawn now, I could see the flashing blue lights of multiple police cars parked at the foot of the building.

Fire engines too, a brace of them, here to make sure the fire was truly out, no doubt, were parked to one side. Their flashing lights spun lazily, creating strobe patterns on the rear façade of Buckingham Palace.

Cassie appeared by my side. 'What a mess,' she murmured, though whether the comment was intended for me to hear I could not be sure.

Lord Edward wept for his brother, kneeling next to the body, and sobbing even though Nugent had tried to kill him and was going to be found responsible for the two murders the dragon had already committed.

Had Lord Nugent been trying to get into the palace to kill his brother but failing each time because he was discovered? It fit the events. He killed a soldier in the grounds, and he killed a member of palace staff when he finally got inside. Defeated twice, he then lied about Edward inviting him, and was able to get into the palace and bring his dragon suit with him. It was in the abundance of luggage he brought along tonight.

How though was he not shot? The material of the suit was gossamer thin. The propulsion unit, a clunky thing on the back hidden by the wings had burned away to nothing. I was struggling to believe that it could work, propelling him around in the air in such an effortless manner, yet it had. Now there was almost nothing left of it to inspect.

I could accept the ability to fly, but how was he not riddled with bullet holes?

And what about the footprints?

It just wasn't adding up.

Approaching voices drew fresh curses from Cassie. She sighed and muttered several unprintable expletives, turning to face the new arrivals.

'That's my boss,' she let me know.

'The one who sent you here when his wife …'

'That's the one,' she confirmed.

'DI Munroe, report,' a voice commanded, drawing my attention to a man in his fifties. He had an air about him – a sense of power perhaps. In his wake, three men in suits and half a dozen uniformed officers trailed. Cassie's boss was tall and handsome – a lot like Raef in many ways though a good two decades older.

Despite their past, I had the instant impression he was not on her side.

'She set fire to the palace, Commissioner,' reported Sir Cuthbert like a tattletale in school. 'And she brought some fool paranormal investigator into the palace without seeking permission first.'

'I don't need permission to recruit specialists,' Cassie retorted calmly.

I stepped forward, hoping I could shift the blame for the fire away from Cassie.

'Good evening. I'm Jane Butterworth. The fire was my fault.'

'I don't care,' snapped the commissioner, shutting me up instantly. 'You've no right to be here and any actions you have taken are the responsibility of DI Munroe.'

The commissioner's face bore a severe frown. He looked like a disappointed father as he turned his gaze back to look down at Cassie.

I wanted to argue but I could not think of anything to say that would change the likely outcome.

'Look, I can see where this is going and how badly you want to make me the scapegoat,' Cassie started arguing. 'I did what was necessary and brought an end to the mystery that has been plaguing the palace for the last week.'

'And in so doing caused the death of a member of the royal family!' snapped Sir Cuthbert, his voice dripping with derision.

'He was inside the dragon suit, sir,' Cassie pointed out. 'I think I can safely argue that he caused his own death. He was trying to kill his brother, Lord Edward.'

'I've heard enough.' The commissioner cut her off. 'Get this … woman,' I've been called worse things, 'back to the palace.' He pierced me with his eyes. 'You will sign the official secrets act before you leave tonight, and you will not breathe a word of this to anyone. Do you understand?'

I blinked, giving myself a second of thinking time. 'You wish to gag me so the truth can be hidden?' I was challenging him, and I'll be honest, with a sea of judgemental faces staring back at me, I was feeling almost as scared as I had when I faced down the dragon.

I also felt righteous. What if I refused to sign? I didn't believe they were going to try to make me disappear.

'Please.' The single word, spoken with an imploring voice stopped me in my metaphorical tracks. 'It will break father's heart to hear that Nugent is dead. Please don't burden him with guilt for favouring me over him,' begged Edward.

He was still kneeling next to his brother's corpse, looking wretched and appealing to me for help.

How was I supposed to say no to that?

An hour later, I was in my car and on my way home. The heating was on full, blasting warmth back into my bones. The cold had penetrated right into me, but I was too caught up in events to really pay much attention to it.

Cassie was going to cop the blame for the fire and expected to be fired from the police. It was grossly unfair. When I asked her about fighting it, all I got was a shrug. She could expose her boss and accuse him of sexual misconduct but to drag his name through the dirt meant dragging her own too and that would impact her parents. Even if she won, Cassie didn't believe she would be able to return to active service.

To distract myself, and because there was nothing I could do to help, I had probed her about the holes in the case.

How had Lord Nugent flown? Where were the bullet holes? Why had he been so willing to leave evidence strewn all over his room on the night he planned to kill his brother?

She had no answers and was too distracted by the events shaping her life to give my questions any thought. I felt sorry for her, but there was nothing I could do to help.

When they sat me down to make me sign away my right to ever speak about the events again, I had no resistance left. That was largely down to Eddie/Lord Chamberlain. There was only one Lord Chamberlain now, and whether he liked it or not, he was now the heir to his father's dukedom.

I flicked my indicator stalk, checked my mirror, and merged with the traffic flowing south out of the capital.

In the morning, I would need to file a report for the business and had no idea what I was going to write. Tempest and Amanda would understand the concept of a gag order – they would just let it go.

I wasn't so sure that I would.

Epilogue. Thursday, October 12th 2258hrs

'You see, Henkel? It really was as easy as I said it would be.' Lord Chamberlain stroked his dachshund's head and down the little dog's back. Henkel's eyes were closed though he was not asleep.

The show had gone entirely to plan. Better than he could have hoped for even. Putting Henkel to one side on his bed, Edward picked up a jar of moisturising cream from the dressing table and began to massage some into his thumbs.

The control rig for the one-off specialist-built drone was murder on his hands. The hours of practice flights to get good enough with the controls to be able to make it move convincingly had left deep welts in his otherwise perfectly manicured hands. A lifetime of privilege ensured baby soft skin that rebelled against the sores he now displayed.

It was worth it though. His brother came when called; Edward extending the olive branch after years of being the one to shun Nugent. That everyone believed him when he claimed it was the other way around and then again when he lied to say he hadn't invited Nugent to the palace, well, it just showed that he was the rightful son to succeed his father.

Subduing his brother and carting him across to the lake had been hard, physical work. So too the run back to the palace to operate the dragon again. That paranormal investigator figured things out quicker than he expected, but it didn't matter.

Or did it?

Edward gave himself a few moments to consider the young blonde woman. There was something unsettling about her and he didn't just mean the oversized hands and feet or Adam's apple. He heard her when she questioned Nugent's lack of bullet holes, and while no one else even thought to question the evidence as presented, she found his footprints from carrying Nugent out to the lakeside.

Rigged with an incendiary device and set to go off at the flick of a switch, his unconscious brother burned to death to make everyone think he had been inside the near-weightless drone. They didn't question it, and though they might search the area, he knew they would never find the real drone sunk at the bottom of the lake.

It was a perfect crime, and he was now one step closer to his goal.

As he screwed the lid back onto the moisturiser, he grinned at himself in the mirror.

'One step closer to the throne, Henkel. One step closer. Father will die in a few years' time, and before he does, I need to knock off the eleven people ahead of him. I rather think Prince Markus' wedding might end in the tragic elimination of at least half of them. Imagine it, Henkel.' He swept the dog up and into the air so they were almost nose to nose. 'All those prominent royals in the same place at the same time and then a terrible accident occurs.'

Edward let go of his dog with one hand so he could cover his mouth as he made a big show of gasping at the horrifying concept.

'It's not like anyone will suspect me. I won't suddenly be the king, will I? Not until daddy dearest dies anyway.'

The End

Except it really isn't. There are more Blue Moons stories to come – you can check out the next one by scrolling down or turning the page.

Plus, there is another story from a different series filling the rest of this book.

Author's Notes

Writing short stories requires a different skillset to producing a sixty-thousand-word novel. Trying to get enough description in to get the story started but keep the balance of the story in proportion is something I struggle with. Writing longer stories is easier in my opinion.

So why didn't I just make this longer and more convoluted? No idea. Story ideas come to me, and I try to capture them. Much like the previous story in this series, which was supposed to be five thousand words and ended up being more than thirty thousand, I start writing with no real idea where the words will take me.

This is an appropriate length for a short story, and it has a purpose which will become more apparent in a few books' time. My series overlap, with many characters from one series appearing in another at some point. A year or so from now, four of my series will collide in a single story surrounding a royal wedding which I mention here.

Jane failed to resolve this case – a first for my Blue Moon series unless you count the five books it took to catch the Sandman – and it will plague her because she knows there is something fishy about Lord Nugent Chamberlain's death.

In this story I touch on the subject of people breaking into Buckingham Palace to take selfies. To my knowledge, that does not happen. However, on July 9th, 1982, Michael Fagin, an unemployed man from London, snuck into the palace grounds, got inside the palace, and made it as far as the Queen's bedroom.

The Queen was asleep in her bed, reportedly only waking when the man pulled back the curtains to let in some light. Thankfully, he had no evil intent for he was alone with the Queen for several minutes before she was able to attract the attention of a maid and escape.

The next book in this series – A Shadow in the Mine – is already started. I need to polish this off tonight while my family is in bed and knuckle down to get it written tomorrow morning. It will take me a good couple of weeks, no doubt, if not longer, though I hope to finish it in nine days.

Theoretically that is plenty of time, but other tasks such as marketing, advertising, liaising with translators, and battling my way through the supply chain to get my books into the high street bookstores, continue to diminish my available writing hours.

However long it takes, I promise to make it fast paced and filled with adventure. I have acknowledged to myself at least, that at some point I will need to put the Blue Moon series to rest – it will soon be twenty books deep. They will always have a special place in my heart though, for they were the first books I wrote and how my author journey came to life. I will admit the concept of ending it troubles me.

I don't want to drag it on and allow the stories to become stale. I have seen that with too many other series written by different authors. I also don't want to just let it peter out and not give the reader a proper ending. How to do that though?

Kill them all? Kill Tempest? Surely not.

I shall have to come up with something, but for the meantime, I have a few stories up my sleeves and will continue to publish a few a year.

Take care.

Steve Higgs

What's next for the Blue Moon Crew?

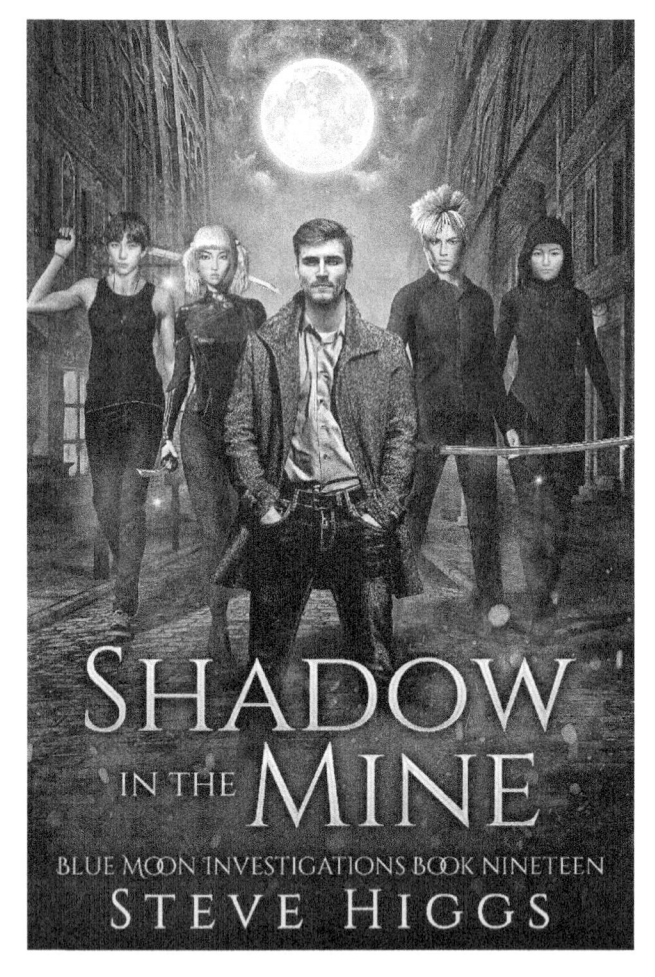

SHADOW IN THE MINE
BLUE MOON INVESTIGATIONS BOOK NINETEEN
STEVE HIGGS

Called to investigate a mystery at a local gypsum mine, paranormal detective, Tempest Michaels, expects to find a rational explanation for the strange events ...

... instead, he discovers a body and a horrified staff.

Recent earth works exposed something ancient, twisted, and above all evil. It has claimed one life already and the staff are terrified for who might be next.

No one saw what it was though, just a glimpse of a shadow.

Why does it want to keep people away from the area? Will it claim more bodies as the mine's owners believe? Or can Tempest unravel the mystery behind the shadow before it can strike again?

One thing is for sure, this is like nothing he's ever faced before, and just maybe this time, the creature is real.

The paranormal? It's all nonsense, but proving it might just get him killed.

Big Apple Pie

An Apple Pie / Patricia Fisher Crossover Mystery Adventure

A Novella

Chelsea Thomas & Steve Higgs

Text Copyright © 2021 Steven J Higgs

Publisher: Steve Higgs

The right of Steve Higgs to be identified as author of the Work has been asserted by him in accordance with the Copyright, Designs and Patents Act 1988

All rights reserved.

The book is copyright material and must not be copied, reproduced, transferred, distributed, leased, licensed or publicly performed or used in any way except as specifically permitted in writing by the publishers, as allowed under the terms and conditions under which it was purchased or as strictly permitted by applicable copyright law. Any unauthorised distribution or use of this text may be a direct infringement of the author's and publisher's rights and those responsible may be liable in law accordingly.

'Big Apple Pie' is a work of fiction. Names, characters, businesses, organisations, places, events and incidents either are the product of the author's imagination or are used fictitiously. Any resemblance to actual persons, living or dead, events or locations is entirely coincidental.

Table of Contents

A New Entry on the Chart. Thursday, October 12th 1812hrs

Royal Targets. Thursday, October 12th 1927hrs

Two Sides of the Same Team. Thursday, October 12th 1934hrs

A Royal Arrival. Thursday, October 12th 2001hrs

A Crazy Plan. Thursday, October 12th 2012hrs

The Younger Brother. Thursday, October 12th 2026hrs

Fire. Thursday, October 12th 2048hrs

Fire at Will. Thursday, October 12th 2055hrs

Evidence. Thursday, October 12th 2102hrs

Stalemate. Thursday, October 12th 2117hrs

It Doesn't Add Up. Thursday, October 12th 2130hrs

Epilogue. Thursday, October 12th 2258hrs

Author's Notes

What's next for the Blue Moon Crew?

Patricia and Barbie

Miss May and Chelsea

Patricia and Barbie: Arriving in New York

Miss May and Chelsea: Visiting Time

Patricia and Barbie: Two Sides of the Same Problem

Miss May and Chelsea: Heading to the Crime Scene

Patricia and Barbie: My Ego Is Bigger Than Yours

A New Team

On the Trail

Luggage Legends

Chased Again

What's in the Box?

Dinner and a Clue

The Man with the Money

Hatchet Men

Dirty Cop

A Secret No One Knows

Rugged Tires

Wolf

New Player

The Sting

Riding Pillion

Epilogue

Author's notes by Steve Higgs

Apple Orchard Cozy Mystery by Chelsea Thomas

More Books by Steve Higgs

Free Books and More

Patricia and Barbie

'What do you mean you have a brother?' I asked the question with complete incredulity because in the months we had known each other, she had failed to mention any siblings at any point.

Barbie cocked an eyebrow in my direction. 'I've talked about him loads, Patty.'

'No. No, definitely not,' I argued, shaking my head. 'I would remember if you mentioned a little brother. How little is he?'

Barbie had her lips pursed and her eyes cast up into her head as she consulted her memory. She was searching for a conversation where the subject came up, but she gave up after a few seconds with a dismissive flap of her hand. My blonde friend, a gym instructor and perfect size zero from California, was hastily packing a bag and that was more important than making a point.

'It doesn't matter,' she relented, accepting that maybe her conversations on the subject might have been with someone else. 'What does matter is that he is in jail.'

My jaw dropped open. 'Jail? What for? Where?'

A handful of underwear from her top drawer got stuffed roughly into the tote bag lying open on her bed and she put a hand to her head as she tried to work out what she was forgetting.

'Passport!' she exclaimed, an index finger in the air as she remembered something vital.

'Barbie!' I all but screeched. She wasn't giving me any answers. We were supposed to be leaving England tomorrow to return to the cruise ship where we both lived and worked, but Barbie clearly had other plans now.

I got the same index finger, held in the air to beg a moment's grace. Her passport was in her handbag, a snazzy Louis Vuitton thing in bright colours that seemed to go with whatever she chose to wear. I would never be able to pull it off, but then I am three decades older and don't look like I fell off the cover of a glossy magazine.

She checked the inside while questions continued to form an unruly queue in my head, then placed it calmly and purposefully on top of her tote bag and turned to face me.

'Bobbie is twenty. He is attending the *Culinary Institute of America* in New York State where he is learning to be a chef. He could have read law or medicine ... he got the brains,' she claimed. Barbie likes to pretend that she is dumb sometimes, playing up to the blonde bimbo stereotype because her name is Barbie, and she looks like a Barbie doll.

She is nothing of the sort.

'He loves food though,' she continued, 'so he is studying that instead. Chances are he'll be the next Gordon Ramsey or something.'

'So what happened?' I begged to know.

Barbie huffed a deep sigh, her shoulders deflating as she slumped to sit on the edge of her bed.

'He and his friend were caught with a body. Bobbie says they found him in an alley when they ducked in to ... they'd had a few beers. Yes, I know, they are underage. Nevertheless, they were on their way to the bus stop and decided they needed to make use of the ... alley to relieve themselves. I guess that's what guys do. Anyway, they found a man and he was bleeding. They tried to revive him, but he ...' Barbie struggled to get the words out and needed a moment to gather herself. 'Bobbie said, every time they tried to pump his chest, more blood spilled out. He said the man had been stabbed several times. When they went for help, they were both covered in blood and the police arrested them both for murder.'

I had my hand over my mouth and my eyes were about as wide as they could get.

'Oh, my goodness!' My mind was racing, trying to take in all that she was telling me while simultaneously starting to form a plan.

'He got his one phone call and chose to call me.' A tear rolled down her right cheek and she swiped at it, angry that her emotions were getting the better of her. 'The stupid idiot picked up the knife.'

I closed my eyes in mute horror. It was a classic mistake.

'According to the police, the man was drinking in the same bar as they were – a place called the Orange Banana Bar. Bobbie says they are not even looking for another attacker even though he and his friend continually protest their innocence. I have to go.'

'To New York?'

Barbie nodded, her lips pursed together tightly in her frustration and worry.

'There's a flight into JFK at 1145hrs. If I can catch that, I can be with Bobbie before evening.'

There was no need for me to even consider what I was going to do.

'Then I'm coming with you,' I stated bluntly and boldly. This was not a subject we were going to discuss.

Barbie opened her mouth to do what anyone would – she was going to tell me I didn't have to do that. She saw the set of my jaw and closed her mouth again.

'Thank you,' she said, her voice soft and quiet. 'I think that's why he called me and not mom, actually. Everyone back home knows about you.'

I nodded, acknowledging that my successes, particularly against The Godmother, had brought me fame of a sort. Notoriety might be a more accurate, if less pleasing term. It came with a burden, but it was one which I carried gladly. If I could help Barbie to prove her brother's innocence, that was exactly what I was going to do.

I was going to New York.

Who am I?

Yes, I suppose I ought to introduce myself. My name is Patricia Fisher. I was a fifty-something bored housewife with little going on in my life and nothing much to look forward to. That is until I caught my husband in a compromising position with my best friend. Not Barbie – this was a different person from a time before I met my current circle of friends.

Long story short, I emptied my husband's bank accounts, ran away on a cruise ship, and woke up accused of murder. I met Barbie that morning and in the aftermath of the murder debacle, I discovered a hidden part of my brain that can unlock clues and solve a mystery like no one else. I managed to prove my own innocence by revealing the real killer – it was all to do with a priceless sapphire someone stole thirty years earlier.

Since then, my life has been one long murder mystery. I could do without the bodies, but my life now has purpose and adventure, and I get to travel the world doing it.

Then there is the captain of the ship, but that is a tale for another time.

I hugged Barbie, attempting to impart that it would all be all right and hurried away to let Alistair, my boyfriend, and Jermaine, my butler, know about the sudden change in plans. Neither would be happy that I was going to leave them behind, but both needed to return to the ship.

Little did I know as I packed a bag in England, the same thing was happening three and a half thousand miles away on the other side of the Atlantic.

Miss May and Chelsea

Have you ever had a staring contest with a suitcase? If not, let me warn you in advance, the suitcase always wins.

Maybe you're wondering, why would someone make prolonged eye contact with an inanimate object? Well, for me, Chelsea Thomas, the answer was simple ... the suitcase wanted to be unpacked, and I didn't want to unpack it. In fact, I flat out refused. Unpacking meant my vacation was officially over, and I wasn't ready to accept that.

Sure, part of me was happy to be home on my aunt's apple orchard, *The Thomas Family Fruit and Fir Farm.* And I was welcomed home by the smell of fresh apple pie, baked by my aunt, Miss May, and taste-tested, repeatedly and with excessive zeal, by her best friend Teeny. Who could ask for more?

But I'd just spent three days at a boutique hotel in New York City with my cousin Maggie. She'd won a free stay in the downtown hotspot, and we'd lived like rich tourists. We'd gone shopping on Fifth Avenue, eaten at swanky restaurants that you just had to know about because there were no signs out front, and we'd walked through Times Square like we were seeing it for the first time. My boyfriend, Detective Wayne Hudson, had even shown up and surprised me in Central Park with one of those cheesy carriage rides. Ugh, I know. So cliché. But somehow, still so romantic.

After such a magical vacation, returning to reality felt like a let-down, and I wasn't ready. So, I was procrastinating by locking eyes with my baggage. But ready or not, reality was on its way into my room, in the form of a bubbly little blonde woman named Teeny.

'Chelsea! Stop whatever you're doing and get in the kitchen!' Teeny looked around the room, and her eyes settled on my unpacked bag. 'Are you just standing here staring at your suitcase?'

'No!' I hung my head. 'Yes.'

'Well stop it! Petey's in trouble and we've got to help.'

Moments later, I was seated at Miss May's big, wooden kitchen table. The mood was serious, and we had serious snacks for a serious problem. Miss May's famous Appie Oater cookies, homemade apple chips, some leftover pie...

Where was I? Right! Petey, a waiter at Teeny's restaurant, had been accused of murder. Apparently, he'd been caught alongside a friend named Bobbie, red-handed next to a dead body in an alley just off East Houston Street. Literally, red-handed. Their hands were covered in blood. Teeny filled us in on the whole story, with lots of wild gestures and a bizarre dramatic re-enactment of Petey trying to perform CPR on a bloody corpse. It was a lot to take in.

'Teeny!' Miss May shouted, around minute four of Teeny's performance. 'We get it. The guy was dead. The CPR was fruitless.'

'No fruit whatsoever,' Teeny agreed. 'And now Petey and this Bobbie character are both in jail. Do you think we can ask Chief Flanagan to help us?'

I choked out a laugh. It was a nice idea – a member of our community was in trouble with law enforcement in the Big Apple, why not turn to our local police chief for help?

Because she hates us, that's why.

Miss May shook her head slowly back and forth at Teeny as her friend bit her lip and wrung her hands.

'I don't think that would work in our favour. Chief Flanagan is as likely to tell them to lock him up just to spite us.'

Why did the police chief of our small town hate Miss May, Teeny, and me? Well, it was kind of a long story. It started with me being left at the altar in New York City, losing my interior design business to my runaway fiancé, and moving back home to the apple orchard to work with Miss May. Then there were some murders.

Okay, a lot of murders.

Together, Miss May, Teeny, and I had stumbled into working as amateur sleuths in Pine Grove, first to protect our own innocence and save the Thomas family farm's reputation. But then we'd sort of just...kept solving crimes before the cops, much to the embarrassment and fury of the actual police department. Sure, Chief Flanagan had legs for days and the shiniest red hair I'd ever seen, but she did not have a winning record as the head of the PGPD.

Either way, she wasn't going to be of any help to us. I didn't say it yet, but I already knew we were going to have to solve this ourselves. My train of thought got interrupted by Miss May talking.

'This is a tough one. I know from my experience as a prosecutor,' Miss May liked to slip in her former career as often as she could, just so no one forgot, 'that it's hard to argue there's no cause for arrest when you catch someone at the scene of a murder covered in the victim's blood.'

'But Petey's not guilty,' Teeny said. 'You know who is guilty? Me!'

'You stabbed a guy in an alley?' I asked.

'No! I scolded Petey for getting an order wrong, because he forgot to say extra cheese on somebody's hashbrown lasagne the other day and I yelled at him and now what if he goes to jail forever and that's the last thing I ever said to him?'

'You could visit him in jail,' I said. 'And also … haven't you already talked to him since then? I thought you were his one phone call and that's how you found out about all this?'

'Oh, don't be a know-it-all, Chelsea!' Teeny crossed her arms. 'Just let me feel bad.'

'If we want to actually help Petey and not just talk about it,' Miss May said, 'then we need to discuss the details.'

'I have a question,' Teeny said, shooting her hand into the air like a kid in school.

'Yes, Teeny,' Miss May said, pointing at Teeny's raised arm.

'Why didn't Petey tell me he had a friend called Bobbie? I've never heard of him. I like to think of myself as sort of a wise elder in Petey's life. He's supposed to tell me everything.'

'Maybe they're new friends,' I hazarded. 'Maybe they just met at the bar in town before they came across this corpse. Who knows? But I doubt they'd been plotting murder together.'

'We didn't have a lot of time to chat on the prison horn,' Teeny said. 'But Petey said this kid's in school at the *Culinary Institute of America.* Maybe Chelsea can pretend to be a student there again, sleuth it up a little.'

In a previous case, yes, I had pretended to take classes at the *CIA*. But it wasn't a role I was eager to reprise. 'No thanks,' I said. 'Let's try just...talking to Petey first?'

'Do we have to?' Teeny said. 'Going to jail is always such a production and it's not like downtown New York is a five-minute drive to get to. I have a shift later.'

Miss May cocked an eyebrow.

'I'm sure this qualifies as a reason to take a little time off.'

'Is it?' I questioned. 'Petey and Teeny are not related. It's not like she's his sister.' I got devil eyes from Teeny and had to raise my hands to stave off her rebuke. 'Hey, I'm just saying. Playing Devil's advocate if you like.'

Miss May nodded.

'Chelsea has a point, Teeny. Anyhoo, whether you come with us or not, we should start this investigation by talking to Petey and his friend.'

Patricia and Barbie: Arriving in New York

Modern flight being the wonder that it is, we were walking through the JFK arrivals terminal less than seven hours after leaving my house in England. To make life easier, and to alleviate Barbie stressing about it, I found and booked our accommodation while sitting in the Gatwick lounge before take-off.

Our hotel was a little pricy, which I put down to the short notice at which I booked it, but it was close enough to where the murder occurred and that placed us right where we wanted to be.

To our right as we exited the building, a taxi rank ten cars deep had more than thirty people waiting. Barbie did what she always does and raised an arm. A yellow cab, on its way to join the back of the rank, screeched to a stop, the driver's eyes locked on the blonde beauty advancing to the kerb.

She might be annoying to go anywhere with because I am instantly invisible beside her and men tend to assume I am her mother, but she does have her uses.

Barbie handed the driver her small suitcase and slid elegantly onto the back seat. I held out my bag, expecting him to take it, yet found I was so invisible the driver closed her door and went around me to reclaim his seat.

He probably would have driven off if I hadn't yanked the door open again. Annoyance wrinkling my brow, I pulled my bag onto my lap and settled in for the journey.

My only experience of New York is from the television. I expected grey buildings towering into the sky like rockets trying to escape the Earth and that was what I got. The streets were narrow, the roads pockmarked and in need of work, and there were neon signs advertising small businesses everywhere I looked.

The car – I had no idea what make or model it was – wallowed in the corners and floated everywhere else. It was like riding a couch and very unlike any of my cars or any car I had ever been in.

Progress was slow, and the driver jabbered the whole-time asking Barbie questions.

'Where are you from? What are you doing in town? Can I pick you up tonight at eight?'

Barbie was polite, but monosyllabic, and the driver got the message in the end.

'This is it?' I asked when the cab slewed into the kerb.

Barbie nodded, her face grim as she stared through the window to the drab, functional building beyond.

In my head, and based entirely on what I saw on TV, I had an image of a glass fronted façade, with bold brushed aluminium lettering and cops bustling in and out. In contrast, what we faced was an old building that was stained with age and had graffiti on it.

It wasn't much better inside.

We sat on hard plastic chairs that were not only bolted together but also bolted to the floor. Was that so they wouldn't be stolen? Or so they could not be turned into weapons? Or both?

People came and went from the front desk area of the station. Filing reports about this, that, or the other, but there was no one else in the waiting area other than two women.

Idly, I observed them. They had a nervous energy about them, much the same as I was feeling in my unsettling surroundings. The younger of the pair had blonde hair that was a little wild. It was hard to work out her height since she was sitting down, but I guessed her age at around thirty. She was lean and attractive, though I could only see the side profile of her face.

Next to her, the other woman was taller and older. She had to be around my age which placed her firmly in her mid-fifties. She turned inward to speak with the younger woman and caught me looking across at her.

We locked eyes for a second until I looked away. Her eyes were a deep blue and there was an obvious intense intelligence behind them.

I had no reason to summarise their appearances, other than it was a habit I'd fallen into. Now employed as a detective on a cruise ship, I was constantly observing people. Both women wore regular day clothes – which is to say hardwearing denim and boots.

In contrast, Barbie and I were both wearing dresses and heels. My heels were short, just enough to give me a confidence boost, but Barbie, who looked like a catwalk model the moment she rolled out of bed, wore a four-inch stiletto. It made her stupidly tall and accentuated her already long legs.

It was a deliberate choice on her part – we used her looks to distract men on a regular basis. You might think it tacky, or degrading, but it sure worked. Men can be such saps sometimes.

After the obligatory wait, which ended just inside sixty minutes, a man in his forties came to find us.

Detective Lieutenant Danvers might have been imbued with energy and passion for his job twenty years ago, but there was no sign of it now. He had a coffee mug in one hand and a sheaf of loose-leaf pages in the other. He looked harassed and weary.

He gestured with his head, 'Come on through, ladies.'

Barbie got to her feet. 'I thought I was going to see my brother?'

Lieutenant Danvers was halfway through the door, slurping coffee and spilling drips on the already stained floor.

'Not before you have spoken to me,' he replied over his shoulder.

We followed him down a long corridor, trailing our luggage on the little built-in wheels until he made a sharp left and shoulder barged through a door. It led to an office, I discovered. The furniture, and décor inside were as dated and tired as the rest of the building.

He thumped a chair as if that was going to make it cleaner, sending a cloud of ancient dust into the air.

'Sorry, girls, only one chair. You'll have to fight over it.'

'You take it, Patty,' insisted Barbie because she didn't want to get her clothes dirty.

Eyeing the dirty, stained material, I made my choice. 'I think perhaps we will both stand.'

Danvers shrugged. 'Suit yourself. The desk sergeant said you just flew in from England and you are a famous sleuth. I thought that was a joke at first.' He sat on the edge of his desk, and twisted his computer monitor - the only thing in the room younger than him - until we could see it.

My face was on the screen. The shot was one taken as we got off the boat in Dublin. The Godmother had just been arrested and the press had been all over us. Barbie's face was just behind mine and a little out of focus.

'I guess he wasn't joking,' Danvers concluded. 'So, given that this is one of the easiest cases I have had this year, I want to know what you are doing here, Mrs Fisher.'

'My brother didn't kill anyone,' Barbie snapped irritably as her worry and stress bubbled over.

Lieutenant Danvers turned his head just a fraction to meet her eyes before saying, 'Yes, he did. You are the phone call then. Barbara Berkeley, Robert Berkeley's sister. I see the family resemblance. No, I'm afraid your brother is guilty. So too his accomplice.'

'Who is that?' I asked, getting in quick before Barbie could start arguing again. The only way we were going to change the cop's mind was by proving without a doubt who did kill the victim.

Lieutenant Danvers bowed his head for a second. When he raised it again, with a sigh of air escaping his nose, he said, 'I am under no obligation to share any information with you. Nor do I believe it is in my best interest to do so, Mrs Fisher.'

Barbie couldn't contain herself. 'But Bobbie is innocent. You must let us prove it to you. We'll do all the work.' She was pleading, her voice about ready to break from the anguish she felt. 'Please.'

The weary-looking cop slid off his desk, put his now empty coffee mug down, and faced us both with hard eyes.

'Look. I have a murder victim in an alleyway stabbed multiple times with a blade also found in the alley. I have two men in custody who were found running from the alleyway with the victim's blood on their hands and clothing. The fingerprints found on the weapon match those of one of the men. The fingerprints of the other are on the victim's wallet. If it wasn't your brother, you would tell me I had the right men and clap me on the back for a job well done. I get it, it's hard. But your little brother tailed a man to an alley where he robbed and killed him. I have the right men and they are going to swing for it.'

Barbie choked back a tearful sob at the detective's choice of words.

'He'll be transferred up state tomorrow morning. Don't waste your time on this one. I don't want to have to arrest you for sticking your noses where they are not wanted. Is that clear?'

It was, but I felt a need to seek clarity anyway.

'You are attempting to instruct us to avoid finding the evidence that will clear their names. Do I have that right?'

Lieutenant Danvers, whose face had been anything but friendly thus far, became a jolly sight darker and less friendly in an instant.

'When I read amateur sleuth, what I see is troublemaker. This is not the right town to be making trouble in. This ain't no cruise ship, lady. You dames need to walk away from this.'

It was a direct threat, subtly delivered.

'May we see Robert Berkeley now?' I enquired politely, a sweet smile tugging at the corners of my mouth.

Miss May and Chelsea: Visiting Time

I kept checking my watch, bored with waiting already. The two women, one of whom had a British accent, had arrived just a minute or two after us, and they'd already been called to go through.

Why were we still waiting?

'Maybe they're here for something else, Chelsea,' Miss May said.

'Maybe, but that's still annoying,' I said.

Another twenty minutes ticked by before a guy in uniform finally stuck his head through a door and called for us to follow him.

'Ahem?' Miss May cleared her throat and held out a hand for me to help her up.

'Oh, you can get up,' I said. I was trying to be empowering, but Miss May stayed with her hand outstretched, waiting. 'Fine, fine, I know, your hips, your knees…' I yanked my aunt to her feet, and we both stumbled a little as she stood.

We were silent as we made our way through the station, the cop leading us along a series of corridors to get to the visitors' area.

'Don't try to pass him anything,' the cop warned with a growl before taking a seat at the back of the room.

The room was split in two by a sheet of Plexiglass that separated the free from the incarcerated. I wondered how the cop expected us to try passing anything to Petey. I guess a person could throw something over the top – there was a gap of about a foot, but I wouldn't trust my aim to get something through that high, narrow opening.

Petey wasn't there waiting for us. I tapped my foot and tried to stay calm as we waited another minute for him to arrive, the sound of keys in locks heralding a door opening in the back wall beyond the Plexiglass.

Even then, it wasn't Petey who stepped out, it was another man. There was a cop right on his shoulder, keeping him in check.

The other man glanced our way, then moved to his right, our left, to a chair at the other side of the room when the cop told him to sit. He had blonde hair and a tan that looked both natural and permanent. Blue eyes sparkled and though he was far too young and beachy for me, I had to acknowledge that the kid was good-looking.

A tap on my arm from Miss May brought my eyes back to the door to find Petey coming through it.

He looked miserable.

No trace of a smile crossed his lips when he spotted us – he just looked small and embarrassed. He tried to walk to the chair opposite us, but the cop caught his arm and held him back.

Petey was getting a talking to, probably the same warnings about what he could and could not do. When finally permitted to do so, he slumped into the chair, snatched up the phone, and sighed a huge sigh like he just didn't know what to say.

'Thanks for coming,' he managed.

Miss May held the phone, angling it away from her ear enough that I could hear him too.

'You look worried,' Miss May said. 'Snap out of it! Tell us everything and we'll figure this out.'

'Yeah, Petey,' I gave him a big thumbs up and a reassuring grin. 'Just snap out of this murder accusation. Nothing to worry about. We'll have you out by nightfall. Or maybe a little later, I just like how nightfall sounds.'

'I sure hope so,' Petey did not sound like he believed me. 'They're sending us upstate to the penitentiary in the morning. That's actual prison, not like Pine Grove jail where everyone likes the mashed potatoes. I don't want to go to actual prison. It feels like I might never come out again once I'm inside.'

He was trying to hold back tears.

Just as Miss May was about to prompt Petey to recall the events that landed him in custody, the door opened behind us, and a different cop walked in. He nodded to his colleague and stepped to the side.

The two women, the Brit and the one who looked like a catwalk model, strolled in. They looked confident, especially the older one. Were they mother and daughter? I didn't think so. The ages were right, but I swear the model had a Cali accent when I heard her speaking.

None of that was important because they were heading for the other kid, the pretty one, and even though Miss May is the sleuth, I could work out for myself that the young beachy kid must be Petey's friend, Bobbie. The model, given how similar her looks were to his, had to be his sister.

Staring at them, I missed what Petey had been saying and asked Miss May to repeat what they had just discussed.

Patricia and Barbie: Two Sides of the Same Problem

We had to wait again, but a uniformed cop came to collect us thirty minutes later. Barbie was vibrating with nervous energy to see her baby brother. There were only two years between them, which given Barbie's fiercely competitive nature, must have led to intense sibling rivalry. I was guessing, but if there had been, it was all forgotten now.

She ran to the plastic chair set opposite a young man with blonde hair the moment we were led into the visiting room. There were three booths, a wooden panel separating each. Perspex, scratched, worn, and displaying doodles, kept visitors from the incarcerated.

Bobbie was already holding the phone to his ear but came to his feet as Barbie rushed to get to him. I could hear her sob as I followed a respectful distance behind.

The two ladies I saw in the reception area were already in the room, crammed into the booth on the left while we had the one on the right. The middle booth was empty, which gave us a modicum of privacy.

Attending catering school with a future in food, I expected Bobbie to be ... well, not fat, but perhaps less perfectly toned and lean than his sister.

He wasn't.

Bobbie Berkeley looked like a fitness model. His naturally blonde hair, like sunshine in a bottle, had been recently cut, the style akin to a military buzz around the sides and back. It was longer on top, his fringe hanging low over his eyes as it swept to the right.

He was muscular in an athletic way, much like his sister and possessed the same intense blue eyes, natural tan, and perfectly white, even teeth.

A different person might have wanted him to be guilty. Not me though. No, I was fine with being the ugly one in the group. Welcomed it even.

I hung back a yard behind Barbie, giving her space so she could unwind some of the tension knotting her insides.

She didn't do that though. She went full big sister.

'How could you be so stupid, Bobbie?' she raged. 'You picked up the knife? What were you thinking?'

'Hi, Sis. Nice to see you too,' he replied. 'Mom and dad are fine, by the way. How are things with you?' He shot her a raised eyebrow that was easy to translate – kindly chill out, stop yelling, and help me.

Barbie sucked in a breath to go again, caught it, and let her shoulders slump as her anger diffused.

'Oh, Bobbie. Do mom and dad even know?'

He shook his head. 'I haven't told them.' He flicked his eyes away from his sister to look at me. 'Is this Mrs Fisher?'

I gave him a wave. I couldn't get to the phone and wasn't sure if he would hear me through the Perspex.

Barbie said, 'Look, don't worry. Just give us as much detail as you can, and we will take it from here. Patty will have this solved in no time.'

Bobbie sank into his chair. 'I sure hope you are right, Barbie.' He leaned his chair back, tipping it at an angle on the back legs. 'Hey, Petey.' His mouth was away from the phone so I couldn't hear him now and was having to rely on lipreading – something I have no talent for – to work out what he said. 'Tell your folks not to worry, brah. My sister and her friend are detectives with mad skills. They will figure out who the killer is and get us out.'

He held up his free hand, making a strange sign with it that involved his thumb and pinky finger sticking out as he wiggled his fist. I tried it. My fist looked like a bull – sort of.

Dismissing it, I discovered the two women talking to Petey – there could be no further question that was the identity of the other young man behind the Perspex – were no longer paying him any attention. They were looking at me instead.

Barbie leaned forward to see around me and waved gamely at the two ladies staring back at us.

'Hello,' she called. 'I'm Barbie, this is Patricia Fisher, you probably heard of her.'

The women exchanged a glance.

'She's who?' asked the younger of the pair.

I couldn't tell if she was feigning ignorance or had genuinely never heard of me. I'm not exactly famous, I've just been in the news a lot recently. I took no insult from her reply.

'Patricia Fisher,' Barbie repeated, then waved a dismissive hand as if the name were not important. 'She's a detective. An English sleuth if you like. A bit like Sherlock Holmes but without the silly hat. That's Bobbie's friend, Peter, right.'

'Petey,' the older woman corrected Barbie. 'Are we listing our credentials now? I have a few of my own.'

'Yeah,' chimed the blonde, 'How about if we solve this case instead? Or first? We're no slouches when it comes to investigating a murder.'

Barbie, demonstrating just how stressed she was, acted out of character, dropping her usual generous nature as her hackles came up.

'This isn't amateur hour, girls. My baby brother is in jail and I'm not going to let you mess up our chance to get his name cleared.'

'We don't mess up, we … get the bad guys to 'fess up,' the blonde said, with a hint of an edge to her voice. 'And we rhyme about it.' She was small but certainly feisty.

Behind me, I noted the two cops were watching the display rather than intervening. They appeared to be enjoying the display, chatting amiably as if watching a show and sharing a drink.

'Bobbie has never been in trouble before,' growled Barbie.

'Chill out, sis,' Bobbie begged through the telephone.

'What are you suggesting?' demanded the blonde. 'You think this is Petey's fault?'

Barbie inclined her head, essentially saying *yes* without saying anything.

'I don't know you and I don't know him, but my brother never got in trouble with the law until he went drinking with your … what is he? Your little brother?'

Bobbie shouted through the phone, 'Barbie!'

I tugged at her dress, trying to get her to calm down but her worry was making her act rashly. I saw the two women here to see Petey as potential allies. They were American for a start – a big help since I knew nothing about the place we found ourselves in. I planned to help Barbie to clear Bobbie's name and would use any resource I could to achieve it. If Petey's relatives could be of help, super.

The older woman locked eyes with me, she appeared to be sizing me up. That intense intelligence was there again. I had no idea who she was, but I got the impression she was nobody's fool.

She reached out to grab the younger woman's sleeve, but the blonde tugged her arm out of reach.

'Petey is as innocent as a ... very innocent person,' the blonde stammered. 'Come on, Barbie doll,' she switched to insulting Barbie in a bid to get her to react. 'If you're implying Petey killed someone, why don't you just say it?'

Barbie wasn't about to be intimidated but sensing that things were about to come to a head, the cops finally pushed off the wall.

'All right, girls. That's enough now,' said one cop, spreading his arms and advancing on Barbie to push her back to my corner. The other cop was doing the same to her opponent.

Both women were hot under the collar and shooting daggers with their eyes as they backed away from each other.

'You've got ten minutes,' advised the cop nearest us.

It was enough to refocus Barbie's attention. We had ten minutes to find out as much as we could. We needed to grill Bobbie for information and get out into New York. This case wasn't going to solve itself.

Miss May and Chelsea: Heading to the Crime Scene

'The nerve of that woman,' I said, still angry at the cops for stopping me before I… well I don't know what I was planning to do to that statuesque blonde. Karate-kick the perfect out of her? I wasn't usually jealous of strangers for being too attractive. That would be crazy. At least that's what I tell myself, but there are some women who just got an altogether too big a helping of *fine* handed to them. And why did she have to be so tall?

Miss May tutted, 'Let it go, Chels,'

'That woman was an actual Barbie! Did you see her blonde hair, and her gravity-defying chest and her waist? I mean how does she even find clothes small enough to fit that thing? She was too pretty to be getting in my face.'

'Bigger fish to fry, Chels.'

We were outside the station and on our way to where Petey said they found the victim. It was less than twenty-four hours ago which meant, according to Miss May, that the crime scene tape would have been stolen and any hope of there being any evidence left to find was nil.

'But why not start at the bar they were in?' I questioned. 'That Orange Banana place? Surely that will yield some clues.'

Miss May just shook her head. 'It will be locked up tighter than Fort Knox. If Kris Wu was killed right outside it and was drinking there before he died, the cops will have shut it until they are sure there is no further evidence to uncover. It might not be shut for long, but there is no hope it is open right now.'

'So we are going to the alley instead?' I wanted to know.

Miss May huffed as she ambled to the curb and stuck out her hand for a cab. 'Yes, Chels. That's our start point. I want to take a look at the place. If Kris Wu,' we'd gotten the name of the victim from Petey, 'was killed there, my first question is, what was he doing in that alleyway? Who willingly goes into an alleyway in New York?'

'Um, drug dealers?' I guessed. 'Murderers? Gangsters?'

'Exactly,' agreed Miss May, making me smile because I thought it might have been a trick question.

Petey had not been all that forthcoming with information which was largely because he didn't know anything. He and Bobbie had met at the Culinary Institute a while back and were out for a beer last night. They had four beers each, left the bar just after ten o'clock to get to the subway, and stopped on the way to pee behind a dumpster when they spotted it from the mouth of the alleyway.

Unfortunately for them, Kris Wu was behind the dumpster, face down and trying to crawl to the street to get help. They tried to help him, but the way Petey told it, the man had to have been beyond saving when they got there.

Bobbie found the knife and was stupid enough to pick it up. Petey found the man's wallet lying just a few yards behind him in a slug trail of blood. He checked it to find out the man's name, nothing more, but his prints were on it, and the police were content to assume it was a robbery gone wrong.

It didn't help that when the cops picked at the boys' story, it turned out they didn't have the money to pay for the subway anyway.

And that was about all we had. The name of the victim, the bar he'd been drinking in, and the location of the place he died – an alley behind a deli just off East Houston Street on a side road called Ludlow.

The cab driver got us there as swiftly as traffic would allow. That turned out to be almost twenty minutes – late afternoon is not the time to try going anywhere in New York.

'This is it?' he asked, ducking his head to check in the rear-view mirror. 'My uncle has a much nicer place right around the corner. I can get you a discount there.' He thought we were going in the deli because that was the location we gave him to go to.

Miss May grabbed her door handle. 'I like this one,' she shot over her shoulder as she slid over the seat and onto the sidewalk.

I was left to pay the bill, handing over a crisp twenty with instruction to keep the change as I checked the traffic and decided to get out on the sidewalk too.

We found the alley, just as Petey described it – behind the deli on Ludlow, but wouldn't you know it? The bubble-headed blonde and her English mother were there already.

Patricia and Barbie: My Ego Is Bigger Than Yours

I was crouching to examine the ground. We had tried to visit the Orange Banana Bar but found crime scene tape strung across the doors. The bar was clearly not open for business, so short of breaking in, which I doubted would work in our favour, we were not going to get to look inside.

Therefore, we were in the alley around the back.

There was little left to show there had been a murder here less than twenty-four hours ago. The crime scene team must have done their job, taken pictures, gathered evidence, and then had a different team in to clear up the blood.

It was better than leaving it on the street for sure.

However, it also meant there was almost nothing left for me to find. Almost nothing. From what Bobbie said, the trail of blood Kris Wu left in the alley went back almost twenty yards – he'd been trying to drag himself into the street where he might be seen and saved.

I guess the crime scene team and the detectives figured they had an easy case with the suspects already in custody because they hadn't searched the alley as effectively as they otherwise might.

'You've got to be kidding me,' muttered Barbie in a sufficiently annoyed way to get my attention. 'Patty, look who it is.'

I stood up, dropping the thing I had just found among the litter on the ground into my handbag as casually as I could, and turned around to see what had Barbie riled again.

'It's that midget and her mom from the cop shop,' she muttered. 'They must have followed us here.'

I was beginning to wonder if Barbie had a point about them getting in the way. I didn't know for sure if the item I had just found was going to bear fruit as a clue to follow, but if they had beaten us here, would they have found it first?

'I looked your mom up,' called the short blonde woman, advancing down the alley with a fierce stride. 'She's just some woman from a cruise ship. My aunt was a distinguished prosecutor. She has a law degree and now she and I solve murders like, all the time. I think we're more qualified to handle this particular situation.'

'I'm not her mother,' I replied, speaking for myself.

'Whatever,' the short blonde said, shooting her green eyes at me for the first time. 'I saw you put something in your purse. If it's some sort of clue, then hand it over, you … out-of-towners!'

'Now then, Chelsea, be polite,' chided the taller woman. Now that I was getting a better look at her, I revised my earlier estimate – she was in her sixties if the lines around her eyes told a story. She was several inches taller than me at maybe five feet ten and what many would describe as handsome – a term for the older woman when pretty just didn't fit anymore.

'Thank you,' I inclined my head.

I got a nod back before the lady said, 'I'm sure these two ladies are willing to use their common sense and give us whatever they found without any need for name-calling and such.'

My eyebrow cocked itself. 'Common sense?'

The older woman offered me an apologetic smile, one that made me think she was attempting to be kind but thought I was being foolish at the same time.

'It's obvious you're not from around here, Mrs Fisher. Yes, I know your name,' she added quickly before I could comment. 'Chelsea is right, we are the locals. And we've solved our fair share of murders. No one is better placed to tackle this investigation. Now, please, hand over whatever you've found. We'll keep you informed if you like.'

'Keep us informed,' Barbie gasped.

The penetrating whoop, whoop of a police siren stopped anyone from saying anything else.

We all shifted our attention to look back to the mouth of the alley where an unmarked police car now blocked the street. I could tell it was an unmarked police car because Lieutenant Danvers was getting out of it.

He did not look pleased.

Through gritted teeth and a grimace, he asked, 'Would you ladies mind telling me what you are doing here?'

I opened my mouth to talk. So too did the tall woman with the dark hair, but neither of us got to answer him because someone started shooting.

The deafening crack of the shot and the zip noise as it whizzed by our heads was followed by another and then another.

I couldn't say if all four of us were screaming, but I definitely was, and my voice was not alone.

'Patty!' yelled Barbie, grabbing my arm and pulling me to the side of the alley by the big trash thingy. Dumpster - my brain supplied the American word for it.

The tiny blonde and the older woman hit the wall too, all four of us sharing the same space and none of us actually safe.

Danvers was firing back, but also trying to get into his car. One thing was clear – he wasn't trying to save us.

A glance around the edge of the dumpster revealed several young Chinese men. They were hunkering against the walls or finding things to hide behind but popping out to fire another shot. I could hear them shouting to each other in their native tongue.

Of course, I didn't understand a word of it. What I did understand was our need to be somewhere else.

'Barbie!' I yelled, flapping my hand behind my body to swipe at her as well.

Her head appeared next to mine.

'Patty!' she yelled back, breathless and excited. 'Why are people always shooting at us?'

Behind her, the other women were shouting something too. I couldn't hear what they were saying, but I had a plan to escape our current confines. It was too far to go if we tried to get back to the mouth of the alley and the security the sidewalk offered. We were on the wrong side of the dumpster too, but we might be able to use it anyway.

I pointed across the alley.

'Over there. Do you think we can make it?'

Barbie shouted, 'I'd rather try than stay here!'

A bony hand grabbed my arm. It was the older woman, I discovered with a twist of my head.

'We need to get out of here!' she shouted to be heard above the sound of guns firing. There were sirens now too, but I didn't know if more police coming would scare the armed thugs off or bring reinforcements. I had no desire to find out.

'Everyone grab the skip!' I screamed, forgetting, in my panic, to give the trash receptacle its American name.

I got a, 'Huh?' and a quizzical look from the short blonde.

Thankfully, Barbie translated for me. 'The dumpster! We're going to roll it across the alley. When they start shooting at it, we make a break for th …'

She didn't get to finish the sentence because a sound like a rocket powered grenade coming down the alley proved to be rather distracting.

A New Team

It was it turned out, in fact, a rocket powered grenade the women all heard, and they got to watch as it shot over their heads. It missed the intended target – Lieutenant Danvers' car – and hit a parked truck on the other side of the street. The effect was fairly spectacular.

Chelsea uttered the first syllables of a shocked swearword before the rest of her sentence was obliterated by the truck's fuel tank exploding.

Patricia's disbelieving eyes didn't get to watch much of the expanding fireball because Barbie had hold of her arm and was running.

Patricia noted, as she flailed along behind her young friend like a flag in a running child's hand, that Barbie also had the short blonde's hand and she in turn held onto the hand of the older woman.

With their heads down and nothing but prayers in their heads, they ran across the alley at an angle to reach a narrow side passage. It was wide enough for pedestrians provided they didn't try to go two abreast.

Patricia gasped for breath, but the older lady, whose name Patricia was beginning to think she really needed to learn, was struggling to keep up at all.

'Can't run,' complained Miss May, wheezing and coughing. 'These legs and hips and knees and lungs aren't what they used to be.'

The ladies were still exposed from the rear. Trapped in the confined alleyway, if one of the armed thugs chose to fire a gun or, God forbid, an RPG, down the alley, they would all be in serious trouble.

'We have to keep going, Miss May,' insisted Chelsea. 'Access your inner jogging strength. Just until we are away from here.'

Barbie, ten yards ahead because she is part gazelle and moves faster than most Olympic athletes, had the solution – what looked like the back door to a bar that she had managed to lever open.

'In here,' she called, gesticulating urgently for everyone to move quickly. Her dress was trashed, and her shoes were gone, abandoned behind the dumpster so she could run at speed, but even with grime on her face, she was still a drop-dead knockout.

Miss May and Chelsea hustled to catch up, Patricia holding back to make sure they got in safely.

The second Chelsea tumbled through the door, Patricia and Miss May slammed it shut, sealing the world, and however many gun-toting Chinese criminals it held, outside.

When a man's voice swore, 'Dang it! I have to get that alarm fixed on that door,' all four women almost wet their panties. Except Patricia obviously who, being English, referred to her undergarment as knickers.

That's probably a moot point though since the effect was largely the same.

Barbie, farthest from the door and thus nearest to the man, turned to find him examining her with a dangerous look on his face and a baseball bat in his hands. The bat looked like it had been used in anger more than once. He sported a bushy handlebar moustache and wore a leather doublet over a denim jacket. The doublet had a badge stitched over his right breast showing the name 'Randy'. He looked like a biker because he was one.

Staring at the four women who just broke into the back of his bar, he allowed himself to relax. It wasn't the first time someone had busted in, trying to steal liquor from his storeroom, but before him were the most unlikely looking thieves he had ever seen. There had been shooting a few moments ago but it wasn't that unusual to hear random gunfire in the middle of the day. It was the explosion he heard which really drew his attention and now he wondered if the dirt-streaked women to his front were something to do with it.

'What exactly are you dames doing? There was an explosion around the corner, are you ladies okay?' he enquired, hiding the bat behind his leg a little as he attempted to pretend it wasn't there.

With a tired laugh, Patricia asked, 'What kind of bar is this?'

The man gave her a single raised eyebrow. 'Not the kind that gets many women who look or sound like you in it.'

Patricia, who had been slumped against the wall, pushed herself upright.

'Let me put that another way. Do you have gin?'

The man consulted the inside of his head, taking a couple of seconds before saying, 'I think I might have something somewhere. I don't remember the last time anyone asked for it. I think the bottle says Hendricks on it?' he said it as a question because he genuinely wasn't sure if that was a brand or not.

Patricia almost choked with excitement.

They were inside Rugged Tires, a biker bar on a back street tucked between Ludlow and Stanton. There was parking for bikes out front and even though it was early evening, the bar had a bunch of bikers in it. They were shooting pool, drinking long necks, and doing nothing to hide the fact that they were eyeing up the women.

Randy led the ladies to a small booth in the far corner of the bar where he wiped the surface down with what appeared to be a soiled rag and took their order. The ladies looked at their surroundings.

The bar was dimly lit, and the floor was old wooden boards with peanut casings strewn across it. There was a path through the peanuts leading to the restroom out back. The clientele all wore derivations of the same outfit, which is to say they were all bikers in denim and leather.

The décor was homemade, currency from around the world stuck to the walls alongside photographs and beermats. It was vastly superior to the alley out back with the Chinese gunmen in it, but they could not have been more out of place if they were foxes trying to get into a chicken only nightclub by wearing red rubber gloves on their heads.

It took less than two seconds for the first would-be suitor to approach them.

'Well, hello, ladies,' he leered appreciatively. His white round neck t-shirt was wet where beer, or perhaps dribble, had found its way to the cotton. His two front upper incisors were missing, and he was fifty if he was a day.

Chelsea aimed her eyes at Barbie, 'I assume he's talking to you.'

'Or you,' the biker corrected her, putting a hand over his mouth to stifle a belch. 'I'm not fussy.' To increase his odds, he added, 'Or one of the older ones for that matter,' he smiled at Miss May and Patricia in turn. 'I'm not fussy.'

Barbie wrinkled her nose. 'Ewww.'

'Leave them alone, Bull,' commanded a voice from a dark corner of the bar. To accentuate his command, the owner of the voice stepped into sight.

Chelsea didn't intend to say, 'Wow,' but the word just slipped out. The man behind the voice was a wonder of nature.

Barbie didn't say anything, but she nevertheless agreed wholeheartedly with the smaller woman's comments.

The man had to be six feet and six inches tall and was built like a linebacker. In jeans, dark t-shirt, and another leather vest thingy, he still looked like he could walk onto the set of an aftershave advertisement and not even need a person to touch up his hair. His face sported a thick covering of dark stubble, and his eyes were like two dark pools of chocolate.

They were the kind of eyes women wanted to stare into endlessly.

Bull bobbed his head and went back to his pool game, acting as if he hadn't even noticed the women were there.

The large handsome man's eyes were still looking their way.

A smile found its way to Chelsea's face. It wasn't intentional – she had a boyfriend, it just sort of appeared of its own volition.

Barbie turned to the table and when she sat down, the tall man blinked and lost interest.

Chelsea muttered something unprintable and plonked her own keister in the chair next to Miss May.

Twenty minutes later, the women knew each other's names and who was related to whom. There were several empty glasses beginning to form a pile on the table between the four women. There was only one topic of conversation.

'Danvers is dirty,' insisted Miss May.

Barbie cocked an eyebrow. 'What makes you think that?'

'Did you hear him call for backup?'

Barbie's mouth made an O shape.

Patricia nodded. 'Good call. I missed that.'

Miss May nodded to acknowledge the compliment. 'Thank you. I used to be a prosecutor here.'

It wasn't the first time that had been mentioned, but Patricia was polite enough to let it pass without feeling a need to make a comment.

'Danvers is dirty,' the British sleuth agreed. 'But what does that tell us? What was he here for? He warned me not to investigate. That makes me think there is something going on that he doesn't want anyone poking their nose into.'

'Oooh, that's what we specialize in,' grinned Chelsea. 'Miss May and I have been solving murders in our town for a long time now. We've been to the city a bunch.'

Barbie lifted her glass for Chelsea to clink hers against.

'We need to include Teeny too,' cautioned Miss May. 'She would not be happy if we left her out.'

'Who's Teeny?' Barbie wanted to know.

Chelsea pulled a face, sucking in a breath through closed teeth as she attempted to find a way to describe her friend.

She plumbed for, 'Teeny is the third member of our team. If you think I'm short, wait until you meet Teeny.'

Miss May chuckled, drawing attention her way. 'Teeny is my age and an absolute firecracker. She's joining us later she hopes, she needed to find someone to cover her shift. It was Teeny who got the call from Petey.'

'We also need to know more about Kris Wu,' commented Patricia. 'I doubt his death was a random mugging gone wrong.'

'Why do you say that?' asked Barbie.

'Because two minutes after we got to the site of his murder, a dirty cop and a gang of Chinese men with guns showed up,' pointed out Miss May. 'Patricia is right, we need to know more about the victim.' She reached across to place a hand on Chelsea's forearm. 'Can you convince Detective Hudson to chase up some information?'

'Who's Detective Hudson?' Barbie asked.

'Chelsea's boyfriend,' answered Miss May without taking her eyes off Chelsea.

'I can give him a call,' Chelsea conceded. 'I probably ought to tell him where I am anyway. We left so fast this morning I forgot to send him a text.'

Chelsea sent a text to get her boyfriend involved and Patricia expressed her relief at having someone from law enforcement on their side. They called stumps on the consumption of gin before they really got a taste for it and were about to start discussing their next move when the door to the bar opened.

The ladies didn't notice the newcomers entering the dimly lit drinking house. Nor did they hear the quiet kerfuffle as the men formed up inside the door pointing ugly, black assault rifles in the general direction of everyone in the room.

The bar's owner, his barmen, and the two dozen biker patrons minding their own business as they supped ale, all saw them though. One barman instinctively reached for his phone, but the sudden appearance of a shiny machete made him withdraw his hand most hurriedly.

The tall, handsome man moved into the centre of the room, his presence imposing. He was silent though, the presence of so many guns enough to deter him from challenging the newcomers.

Now they had control of the bar, the man nearest the door, nodded to his boss who was waiting outside. In contrast to the thugs in their jackets, jeans, and running shoes, Mr Yibo wore a sharp suit. Paired with a fine wool winter coat and a scarf in a clashing colour, he believed he was twenty-first century business elegant.

At the table of women, it was Chelsea who spotted the newcomers first. A colourful word slipped from her lips.

'Chels,' chided Miss May, never a fan of poor language. Then she saw the advancing horde and repeated what Chelsea said – it was appropriate to the situation.

There were more than a dozen armed Chinese men in the bar and they all had the same symbol stitched onto their left deltoids. They were a gang, and the chances were that they were the same gang who shot at Danvers and fired an RPG just a short while ago.

Barbie flinched, bunching her muscles as she looked for a way out. Their only choice was through the backdoor they used to get in.

Seeing her glance that way, Mr Yibo shook his head. 'I wouldn't bother, my dear. I have men stationed in the alley out back.' Seeing their concerned faces, he raised his hands in a bid to instil calm. 'I mean you no harm ladies.'

'You could have fooled me,' commented Miss May.

'Yeah,' agreed Chelsea. 'All those weapons make me think maybe you do mean us harm. Could you put them down? Or just like, aim them a little less … at us?'

Mr Yibo raised an eyebrow in her direction.

'Shutting up now.' Chelsea mimed zipping her mouth closed, locking it, and throwing away the key.

'What is it that you do want?' asked Patricia, doing her best to keep the nerves she felt from affecting her voice.

Mr Yibo nodded, pleased that he was able to get so swiftly to the point.

'I want the marker, ladies. Hand it over and you may go on your way.'

Patricia glanced at the three women sat around the table – all looked equally mystified. Certain her response would not be well received, she asked, 'What marker?'

Anger flashed across Mr Yibo's eyes. 'I must caution against attempting to keep it from me, ladies. It will not be beneficial for your health.'

Miss May spoke up. 'Honestly, we don't have a … a marker. What is that anyway? Do you mean, like a dry-erase marker?'

The gang boss in his sharp suit turned his head to one side and spoke in rapid Chinese to the man closest. He got a single word answer and a shake of the man's head.

'Very well,' Mr Yibo brought his attention back to the table of women as he switched back to English again.

'You just came from the police station where I know you spoke with the two young men who killed Kris Wu. I know they were not found to have the marker in their possession so they must have stashed it somewhere after they killed him.'

'They didn't kill him!' blurted Chelsea. Drawing the scary-looking boss's attention once more, she mimed zipping her mouth shut again, got halfway across her lips, and mimed opening it so she could speak. 'Sorry, my mouth gets carried away sometimes. I babble. I'm famous for it in my hometown.' She zipped up again, thought of something else and ran her finger back to the other side of her mouth. 'Like when I'm nervous. That's the worst time. Just can't keep my mouth shut or my foot out of my mouth.'

'Chels,' Miss May nudged her arm.

Chelsea zipped her mouth shut for a final time and left it that way.

After checking Chelsea wasn't going to say anything else, Barbie reaffirmed what she said. 'The two men in custody did not kill Kris Wu. They found him and were trying to help.'

Mr Yibo's head dropped a little as if the muscles in his neck had unexpectedly deflated. When he brought his eyes back up, they were cold and hard.

'Kris Wu was in possession of a marker which he stole from me. It was not on his body and not among the possessions recovered from your friends when they were arrested. Therefore, the two boys who followed him into the alley last night, stashed it somewhere.'

Patricia gripped Barbie's arm to hold her back from arguing. Miss May did likewise with Chelsea though she truly wanted to argue herself.

'Tell me, ladies, if it was not to retrieve the marker, why did you go to the alley immediately after visiting your friends?'

Prompted to speak, Patricia and Miss May exchanged a glance, both politely offering to let the other speak first.

Seeing them hesitate, Barbie said, 'We want to know who killed Kris Wu so that we can clear my brother and his friend's names. They didn't kill him, and I doubt they know anything about a marker. What is it anyway?'

It being the second time they had asked him the question, Mr Yibo chose to answer.

'The marker is nothing more than a token that represents an amount of money. You can think of it much the same as a casino chip.' He leaned a little closer and lowered his voice to a dangerous growl when he added, 'It's how those of us involved in organised crime move money without needing to move physical money.'

Patricia asked, 'What does it look like?' and got a signal from Miss May that she now understood what they were discussing.

'Enough questions,' snapped Mr Yibo, stifling any further chance of conversation. 'Your friends are to be moved to the state penitentiary at nine o'clock tomorrow morning. You will bring the marker to me before that time or neither will live beyond their first hour there.'

'What!' blurted Barbie, her heart rate rising to a desperate level as she started to hyperventilate. 'But we …'

'Nine o'clock tomorrow!' Mr Yibo raised his voice. 'Or do you require additional motivation?'

The man with the shiny machete came forward, dropping his assault rifle to hang from its strap so he could wield the large knife more effectively. The exact nature of the threat was unspecified and probably best left that way so far as the ladies were concerned.

No one said anything for several seconds.

'Nine o'clock tomorrow morning,' Miss May confirmed their understanding.

Mr Yibo nodded. 'Good. I am glad you see the sense in cooperating.' Another nod of his head carried an unspoken command for his men to withdraw. Silently, they reversed back to the door and out into the street, a man holding the door for Mr Yibo to leave.

In the street, a large Chinese man wearing a heavy jacket and sunglasses even though it was dark, opened the rear door of a blacked-out Bentley.

The large handsome man and many of the other bikers followed them out, saving some face perhaps after having their territory invaded.

Patricia, Miss May, and their younger friends watched through the window, barely daring to breathe until the last armed man left the bar, the door swung shut and the cars outside pulled away.

As Mr Yibo's car cruised down the street, flanked front and rear by two cars each side, the unmistakable roar of motorcycle engines roared into life – the bikers were following, making sure the Chinese went back to their part of town.

'Do you mind telling me what that was all about?' demanded the bar owner, glaring at the four ladies he expected zero trouble from. 'First you break in through my back door. Then a cohort of Chinese gangsters show up in my bar and threaten all my customers. I think maybe it's time you left.'

Miss May spoke for the group. 'We are very sorry.' There was no point protesting their innocence. They might not have invited the organised crime boss and his lackies inside, but they came because they were there anyway.

'This place is going to the dogs, Randy!' shouted an old man at the bar, his comment clearly addressed to the owner. 'That's two nights in a row there have been Chinese in here.'

Halfway to the door, Patricia paused to question what she had just heard. 'I'm sorry, what was that about there being Chinese men in here last night?'

'I said out, ladies,' insisted Randy, the bar owner, walking behind them to make sure they got the message.

As they were ushered out of the door and into the streetlamp light outside, Patricia strained her ears to hear the old man explaining the previous evenings events to the man sitting one along.

On the Trail

On the street outside the bar, the four women took a moment to regroup and work out what to do next.

'Did you notice how the gang boss was acting?' Miss May posed her question at the British sleuth, keen to see how good she was.

'He looked worried,' supplied Patricia without needing to think. 'And if I read his facial cues correctly, he was lying.'

Miss May agreed. 'Lying about what though?' she asked.

All Patricia could do was shrug. 'If we knew that ...'

Barbie fretted, 'We only have fourteen hours, girls.'

Patricia placed a hand on her shoulder attempting to impart some reassurance. 'It will be enough time, Barbie. We've never failed before.'

'It was never my brother before,' Barbie wailed in return.

Chelsea turned to Miss May. 'What else did you see? I was too busy zipping and unzipping my lips to notice anything good. I was counting on you to spot any clues.'

'Not this time, Chels,' she sniffed. 'There really wasn't much to see. But,' she swivelled on her heels to face Patricia, 'I do recall a certain someone picking something up in the alleyway. What did you find behind the dumpster?' She had opted to be gracious in the bar and let the British woman reveal what she found of her own volition.

To be fair, they got interrupted before she could, but if Patricia didn't 'fess up now, Miss May was going to get uppity.

Patricia flipped her eyebrows – the thing she found had completely slipped her mind. Holding her handbag open with one hand, she rooted through the detritus at the bottom with her other. Finally hooking it with a fingernail, she withdrew her hand into the streetlight to show her find.

Barbie, Chelsea, and Miss May all leaned in, squinting at the object in Patricia's palm. It was a small piece of thin white card. Roughly the size of a credit card, it had a barcode in the bottom left corner and above it an emblem and a name 'Luggage Legends'. It also displayed the victim's name 'Kris Wu' in the bottom right corner along with the time and date the card was printed.

No one missed that it was only just over twenty-four hours old.

'What is it?' asked Barbie, fishing for her phone to look up the firm's name.

Miss May provided the answer first. 'It's a place to leave your luggage. In the days before terrorists, there were banks of lockers in Grand Central. Now there are none, but people still need to leave their luggage somewhere and Luggage Legends is one of the firms operating that type of service. They're located right inside the terminal.'

Chelsea frowned at her aunt. 'How do you know that?'

Miss May grinned. 'I know lots of things, Chels.'

Patricia looked at the card. 'So basically, this is a key to a locker in Grand Central. That's kind of a cliché, don't you think?'

Barbie shrugged. 'My feet are getting cold,' she remarked. Then, as if only just realising what had happened, her hands shot to her mouth. 'Oh, my goodness!'

'What?' gasped Chelsea, looking around for danger.

'We left our luggage in the alleyway!'

As you might expect, there was no sign of it now. Both her suitcase and Patricia's were stolen four seconds after the echoes of the last bullet faded to nothing.

Looking down at her ruined clothes, and across at Barbie's bare feet, Patricia sucked some air between her teeth and fished out her purse.

'I guess we need to go shopping.'

No one wanted to delay getting on with the investigation – there was too much on the line – and they agreed sticking together was the best plan, but as Miss May pointed out – there were shops to be found all around Grand Central.

'Where are you guys staying?' asked Chelsea. They had returned to East Houston where Barbie needed less than eight seconds to flag down a cab.

Over her shoulder, as she opened the cab door, Barbie replied, 'The Credenza on Times Square. Not that we got to check in yet.'

Miss May frowned. 'Are you seriously rich?'

Barbie chuckled. 'Patty is. Aren't you, Patty?'

Blushing slightly as the taxi merged with traffic, Patricia shook her head. 'No, actually I am not rich at all. I have a paid job and earn a wage like most other people.'

Miss May wasn't willing to let this one go. The Credenza was one of the biggest, swankiest, and above all most expensive places to stay in New York.

'The cheapest room rate at the Credenza is over a thousand dollars a night. So you're either rich or terrible with your money.'

Patricia blushed again, casting her eyes out the taxi's window rather than meet Miss May's questioning look.

Barbie answered for her. 'Patty saved the Maharaja of Zangrabar's life and restored him to his throne. Now he insists on being her benefactor. The Maharaja has quite a bit of money to spare, so Patty can have anything she wants.'

Chelsea's eyes were wide like saucers. 'That sounds like a pretty sweet deal. You didn't have to uh, offer him anything else? Like promise him your hand in marriage or bump uglies with him first?'

Patricia had never heard the phrase 'bump uglies' before but was worldly enough to work out what it meant.

'Certainly not,' she choked. 'He's a teenager for a start.'

'Lots of teenage boys like an older woman,' argued Chelsea. 'Kids have a word for hot, mature women. A few words, in fact. There's cougar, and—'

Miss May nudged her niece with an elbow. 'Chels.'

'Yes, shutting up now.' Chelsea almost did the zipping her mouth thing again but refrained because the cab was pulling up outside the rail terminal already.

Luggage Legends

The first thing they did was find new shoes for Barbie. She ducked into the first shop they found and came out just a couple of minutes later wearing a new pair of running shoes. They didn't really go with her elegant dress, but somehow she still made the combination work.

Patricia needed a whole new outfit - her clothes were grimy from ducking bullets in the alley, but she insisted it was something that could wait, and no one argued.

Now was not the time for shopping.

Grand Central Terminal was busy, but no busier than any other evening. Tens of thousands of commuters were making their way through the building, each with their own sense of direction and purpose.

Trying to get through the press of people, the four amateur sleuths bumped and collided and had to dodge children, old ladies with dogs, and a luggage train that forged an easy path as it beeped continually, and people moved out of the way.

The Luggage Legends place was easy to find – it had a sign above it that was thirty feet across and visible from any point inside the building.

'Is it suspicious if we all go?' asked Barbie.

'I can do it,' offered Chelsea. 'I have an innocent face.'

'Ha!' cackled Miss May. 'Your face has trouble written all over it, Chelsea. I'll go.' Remembering her manners, she added, 'Unless Mrs Fisher wishes to contest me for the honour.'

Patricia waved her off. 'No, please.'

Chelsea, Barbie, and Patricia then got to watch as the tall figure of Miss May crossed the final twenty yards to the counter beneath the Luggage Legends sign where she attempted to exchange the card for whatever had been left there.

Would it be a large suitcase? Would it be more than one? Would it be the mysterious marker the Chinese gang boss wanted?

When Miss May turned around and began to amble back their way, what they saw in her hand was a briefcase. It was a new, yet nondescript, black briefcase with a handle on top. Patricia found herself questioning when she last saw one in that style. The answer, she surmised, was not for many years.

However, she did not get to dwell on the matter. Nor did she get to find out what was in the briefcase, for Barbie and Chelsea were both grabbing her arms.

Barbie squealed in her left ear, 'I think I just spotted Lieutenant Danvers!'

On Patricia's other side, Chelsea was attempting to tug her out into the open to close the distance to Miss May. 'That's not all! The Chinese are here too! They must have followed us!' she shouted, pointing across the station with a wild arm.

Patricia tracked her eyes where she thought Chelsea wanted her to look and sure enough, there were two Chinese men and when she looked at them, they saw her and started running.

'Quick, Miss May!' Chelsea hooked her aunt's arm and swung her around to head away from the Chinese gang members.

Barbie blocked her route.

'Danvers is coming!' she nodded her head as surreptitiously as possible to show where he was.

Patricia's heartrate was climbing. She hated being chased. She hated it just about as much as being shot at. At least when people shoot at you, you don't have to get all sweaty and out of breath. Nevertheless, it was running time again.

She picked a new direction – the only one they had left – and yelled, 'Leg it!' as she took off.

Miss May, still holding the briefcase, found herself dragged along by Chelsea and Barbie, her feet barely touching the ground as they attempted to evade the Chinese gang members from the left and the dirty cop converging from the right.

Neither interested party heard Patricia's shout – there was too much background noise for that, but they saw Patricia break into a run and spotted the younger women hauling the eldest member of the party after her.

They gave chase and it did not require a keen intellect to calculate they would catch their quarry long before the ladies could get to the nearest of the building's exits.

When Patricia glanced over her shoulder, she knew it too. However, this wasn't Patricia's first time being chased. Not by a long shot, and she had learned a few tricks along the way.

'If in doubt,' Patricia puffed as she ran. 'Cheat.'

Chased Again

Chelsea's phone rang, vibrating in the back right pocket of her jeans as she ran. Hooking it out with one hand to check who was calling, she thumbed the answer button and pressed it to her ear.

'Not the best time, Wayne. Can I call you back?'

At the other end of the line, Detective Wayne Hudson frowned. He could hear Chelsea's breathing. Why was she out of breath? There could be a number of reasons, and he didn't like any of them. Adding it to the details he found on the man she begged him to look up, he found a worrying trend.

'Chelsea what are you mixed up in? I know you wouldn't be running unless something was wrong.'

'I run! I work out! Sometimes. Ugh, I don't have time for this, Wayne. I'll call you back!' Chelsea stuffed the phone into her back pocket again and checked over her shoulder. 'They're gaining!' she squealed.

The Chinese gang guys were coming up fast. Still ten or more yards behind them, they were going to catch her, Barbie, and Miss May in the next thirty seconds. Danvers was about the same distance away but coming from a different direction. It didn't look like Danvers had seen the Chinese yet and vice versa.

Chelsea was about to ask if Miss May or Barbie had any ideas when the beeping sound of an oncoming luggage truck parted the crowd right in front of them. Sitting in the driver's seat and yelling at them as she careened to a stop was the crazy English sleuth!

Patricia screamed, 'Get on!' and not without cause because she had the luggage truck driver and station security chasing her.

The rest of the luggage carts were unhitched so it was just the little golfcart looking thing, but without the towed weight to slow it down, the vehicle was actually kind of sporty.

Miss May's feet were barely on board when Patricia mashed the pedal. If the cart had bucked any harder when it took off, it might have popped a wheelie.

Weaving through the crowd, all four women screaming for everyone to clear the way, and beeping the little horn as frequently as they could, they left Danvers and the Chinese gang members behind. The appearance of station security helped to dissuade the dirty cop and the armed criminals from following, but for the ladies, they were still not out of the woods.

'They've got radios,' yelled Chelsea. 'They'll call ahead and cut us off!'

'I know,' Patricia yelled over her shoulder, her focus on not running anyone over. 'We need to ditch this fast before they get coordinated. Did we lose Danvers and the Chinese?'

'Yes, Patty!' shouted Barbie, standing high on top of the cart to scan ahead.

The danger now was in getting caught by the station security guys. If that happened, they would get handed over to the local cops and the time they needed to save Bobbie and Petey would get eaten up explaining themselves.

Barbie spotted what she was looking for, swung around and down from her place hanging onto the side of the cart to get to Patricia in the driver's seat, and pointed off to the left.

'Over there, Patty!'

What she found was an exit that led into the crowded street outside but did not currently have security guards standing next to it.

Ten more seconds of frantic driving, beeping, and yelling brought them close enough to abandon the cart.

'More running?' complained Miss May. 'Usually, Chelsea and I are the ones doing the chasing. Well, Chelsea is. I'm there for moral support. We're rarely the ones getting chased!' she yelled as they ran through the doors and down some steps to merge with the crowd outside.

Patricia huffed out a breathless laugh. 'Really? Barbie and I get chased all the time.'

'And shot at!' added Barbie.

There was no more time for swapping stories, the security guards would exit the building any second. They had a small window and needed to make good their escape.

Thankfully, that proved easier than expected. Grand Central Terminal, serviced by numerous lines of the Metro system had convenient stairway access to the underground system all over the place.

Out of sight by the time they got six steps down, they slowed their pace and let Miss May get her breath back.

'Where are we going?' asked Barbie forging ahead to keep everyone behind her moving.

'It doesn't matter,' Chelsea raised her voice to be heard and cursed the crowded city. Life was so much simpler, and nicer, in Pine Grove. 'Let's just jump on the first train going downtown.'

Miss May agreed. 'Let's catch our breath and see what's in this briefcase. That's what we came here for after all.'

What's in the Box?

The briefcase was locked, but lazily, Kris Wu, or whoever dropped it off at Luggage Legends, left the combination at the factory set to three zeroes. It was Miss May's first guess and the locks snapped open with a tantalising click.

She gripped the top lid and raised her chin to look at the three companions all gathered close to peer inside.

'Ready?' she asked.

'Get it open already,' Chelsea said. 'Sorry. I'm just hungry. All that running. Open the case though, pretty please.'

Chuckling to herself, Miss May lifted the lid and all four women stared at the contents.

Barbie stuck out her bottom lip. 'Well, that's disappointing. I was expecting a stack of cash, and a gun. Or maybe some diamonds and a severed ear.'

'Ewww,' Chelsea recoiled.

Grimacing, Barbie apologised. 'Sorry. I'm not sure where the severed ear idea came from. I guess I was expecting more than this though.'

The interior of the briefcase was almost entirely empty. The sum total of its contents was a single white envelope. On the front face was a name 'Liu'.

'Do you think maybe that's Kris Wu's girlfriend or his wife?' asked Barbie.

'Dang it!' Chelsea sighed, digging around in her jeans to get to her phone. 'I just remembered that Wayne called,' she explained. 'That was ten minutes ago, and I cut him off. He's probably going to be worried. And upset. Maybe he's assumed I'm dead and already moved on to date Chief Flanagan. I bet she can talk on the phone while running.'

'Oh, I wondered who called you,' said Miss May. 'Did he find out anything about Kris Wu?'

Chelsea chewed her lip – no signal. 'I'll have to get above ground again to find out. Sprinting through Grand Central to avoid a gang and a crooked cop did not seem like the optimum time for taking notes.'

Bringing the group's attention back to the envelope, Patricia said, 'We need to open that. If there is a chance what he says inside can tell us what happened to him, we need to read it.'

Miss May didn't like opening mail addressed to someone else, but Patricia was right, and the circumstances justified it. Using a careful fingernail, she levered the flap open and withdrew the pages inside.

There were two and they were written in Chinese.

'We're going to need a translator,' Miss May huffed.

Chelsea shrugged. 'Anyone else hungry?'

Dinner and a Clue

Killing two birds with one stone, they found a Chinese restaurant half a block after exiting the Metro onto Lafayette Street. The waitress who took their order was happy to get a fifty-dollar bill tip up front to translate the letter for them and promised to have it back to them by the time their food was served.

Chelsea made good use of the time to return her boyfriend's call and set it face up on the table in their booth with the speaker enabled so everyone could hear.

'Chelsea,' Detective Hudson answered the call in a monosyllabic manner. The single word somehow managed to sound concerned and icy at once.

'Hi, Wayne,' Chelsea tried to bluster past hanging up on him earlier. 'I'm with Miss May and some new friends in Manhattan. I have you on speaker,' she warned before he could say anything too personal.

The four ladies heard a sigh come through the phone. 'Dare I ask what you are doing in New York, Chelsea? Does this have anything to do with Teeny borrowing a car from Big Dan and leaving town in a hurry?'

Miss May hitched an eyebrow, wondering why Teeny would borrow a car – she had her own pink convertible.

'Um, I think Teeny is on her way here,' said Chelsea. 'I guess you didn't hear – we had to react fast, but Petey got himself arrested for murder last night.'

'Murder?' blurted the detective. 'In New York?'

'That's right,' replied Chelsea. Everyone else was keeping quiet so she could talk. 'He didn't do it. Obviously. Miss May and I are here to prove it and get him out.'

Wayne was quiet for a few seconds before he spoke again. 'Okay, so what is this Kris Wu guy's connection? You know he's a card-carrying member of the Fou Chin Clan, right?'

Patricia couldn't help herself. 'The who?'

Miss May butted in. 'Sorry Wayne, we need to do some introductions. With us we have an English woman named Patricia Fisher and her friend Barbie from California. Barbie's brother was with Petey when they got arrested. We're trying to get them both out.'

Patricia tried again. 'Hi, this is Patricia. You said Fou Chin Clan? I haven't heard of them. I thought almost all organised crime got wiped out a month ago when the Alliance of Families were arrested around the planet.' Patricia felt no need to comment on her part in that victory.

Miss May silently acknowledged the Englishwoman's modesty. She and Chelsea had looked Patricia up when they left the police station – Patricia Fisher was credited by the press for single-handedly taking down the Alliance of Families organisation and the resulting arrest of almost ten thousand criminals worldwide.

Detective Hudson scratched an itch on the back of his head.

'Well, you are right about the Alliance of Families, but all that really did was create a power vacuum. New gangs are stepping up to fill the void and not every organised crime family on the planet fell under the Alliance of Families' control.'

'But the Fou Chin are new?' Patricia tried to clarify.

'That is my understanding,' Wayne replied. 'Honestly, it's not really my area. I'm just a small-time local detective,' he admitted.

Chelsea was keeping happily quiet since the conversation had steered away from what she was doing in New York and why she was mixed up in gang murders. Unfortunately, though Patricia had momentarily distracted her boyfriend, that didn't last long.

'Shall we circle back to the part about why Chelsea is investigating the murder of a Chinese mafia scumbag?' Wayne pressed for an answer.

Miss May put her hand over Chelsea's and answered for her. 'It's like we said, Detective Hudson. Petey is in trouble, and someone needs to get him out of it. It's not like we could turn to you for help, we are way outside of your jurisdiction.'

While the others conversed, Barbie got online. Her first search was for the Fou Chin Clan. When the first hit showed her the gang symbol, she turned her phone around for all to see.

Patricia, Chelsea, and Miss May all understood what it meant. The symbol on Barbie's phone was the same one Yibo's men all wore, and that meant Kris Wu was one of his.

Detective Hudson didn't argue about the jurisdiction thing; he knew they were right. However, he wasn't content to let things sit as they were.

'I want you to contact local law enforcement there. Tell them what you think you know and leave the investigation to them. These gangs are not to be messed with.'

Chelsea let her mouth off the leash. 'And what, Wayne? Us poor girls might get into trouble? You think we need a man to look after us?'

'I think you're going to get into trouble, yes, Chels,' he replied without rising to her bait. 'It's not like it would be the first time now, would it?'

Chelsea poked her tongue out at the phone, making Barbie snigger.

Barbie was busily trying to find information on Kris Wu, but wasn't getting very far – apparently gangsters don't do social media. She tried the direct approach instead.

'Hi, um, Wayne. This is Barbie. Can you tell us anything about Kris Wu other than that he is dead and was a member of the Fou Chin Clan?'

Detective Hudson sighed. The right thing to do, he knew, was to refuse to divulge any information the women might be able to use to further their investigation. However, doing so wouldn't stop them, they would charge blindly onwards probably tripping over gang members in their bid to find out what he could tell them right now.

For the next five minutes, and with all four women listening, he read through Kris Wu's arrest record and file. He was a third-generation American citizen and the son of a man who worked his whole life as a hairdresser. Aged thirty-four, his record read as that of a man who had been seduced into the gang life at an early age. There was an address for him which Wayne refused to give them on the grounds that his gang friends were bound to be watching the place or living nearby. The final piece of news was one that surprised the group of ladies.

'He's married?' Chelsea asked.

Wayne shrugged, not that anyone could see it, so added, 'Gang members are just like everyone else. They get married, they have kids. You could even say they have careers with promotions, although it's kind of a twisted way to view the world.'

'How many kids?' asked Barbie, hating that there were now more fatherless children in the world.

Wayne checked the file again. 'It doesn't say.'

Further conversation was stalled by the arrival of their food. It was the same waitress who took their order, and she had a notebook sticking out of her pocket along with the original letter they paid her to translate.

Quickly, Miss May snatched up Chelsea's phone and thumbed the button to take it off speaker. 'Is there anything else, Wayne? We have to go.'

'Yes, I'd like a word with Chelsea in private if I may.'

Miss May thrust the phone at her niece, saying, 'He wishes to talk to you. You might want to take it outside.'

Chelsea's cheeks reddened as she slipped from the booth to talk more privately across the other side of the restaurant, and that left the three ladies at the table staring expectantly at the waitress.

She had plates in either hand. 'The kung-po king prawn?' she asked, no longer able to remember who had ordered what.

Miss May's eyes flared. 'Never mind all that. Just put the plates down and we'll sort it out. Please tell us what was in that letter.'

The young waitress leaned back a little, scouting around to see if her manager was watching, then schooched into the empty seat Chelsea left. The women all leaned in toward the centre of the table in a conspiratorial manner.

They were all ears.

'Well,' the young woman started. 'It's a bit sad, actually.'

'How so?' asked Miss May.

'It's from a man to his wife and to his baby daughter, but it is written as if he will be dead by the time they read it. I saw this sort of thing on a film – it was about soldiers writing letters to their wives on the eve of battle. If they died, the letter would be sent home.'

Barbie tried hard not to curl her lip upward. 'A message from beyond the grave.'

Zhou Li, they learned the waitress's name, read her transcript word for word. There could be no doubt Kris Wu believed he was in grave danger because his letter started with "If you are reading this, my darling, I was not careful enough and I am no longer with you." It went on to explain that he had made provision for her and their daughter, and how sorry he was that he never got to see her.

'He never got to see her?' questioned Barbie, failing to follow.

'Yes,' explained Zhou, 'She is travelling to America from China. He also tells his wife, her name is Liu, to take the marker to a man called Freddie Lee and he gives an address.' Zhou turned the page around to show them. 'It's on Hester.'

Barbie pulled up a map on her phone. 'That's only a few blocks from East Houston where Kris Wu was killed.'

'He was killed!' squeaked Zhou.

'Oh, yes,' Miss May made an apologetic face. 'We probably should have mentioned that bit. We're investigating a murder,' she explained.

Zhou's face crinkled a little. 'Are you … cops?'

'Licensed investigators,' replied Patricia before anyone else could think to speak. She was stretching the truth only slightly.

Miss May and Patricia were both deep in thought, each trying to add up what they had just learned and trying to make sense of the puzzle. However, what Zhou said next snapped them both back to the present.

'Can you say that again?' prompted Patricia.

Zhou gave the women a surprised look but did as they asked, 'Do you think this is to do with the marker everyone is talking about?

Patricia glanced across the table at Miss May before asking, 'What are they saying?'

Zhou checked about for anyone listening once more before lowering her voice. 'I heard it from my boyfriend. He's got a couple of friends who are … well, they are not exactly law-abiding, shall we say. Apparently, there is a high-price marker, and everyone is looking for it.'

Barbie scrunched up her face in a confused frown. 'I still don't get how this marker thing works,' she complained.

'Neither did I until my boyfriend explained it,' admitted Zhou. 'Freddie Lee is a loan shark and a financier – I know that much. He is someone who holds and controls money. The marker will have a number on it that corresponds to an entry in a ledger and only the person in possession of the marker can retrieve the money Freddie Lee is holding.'

It was like a beam of light shining through the window to illuminate their heads. Suddenly, they all got it. Danvers, Yibo, anyone else who knew about it … they all wanted the marker because it would instantly net them a pile of cash. Yibo claimed Kris Wu stole the money from him, but even at the time, Patricia believed he was being convenient with the truth. Kris Wu was one of Yibo's men so it could be true, or it could just be that Yibo knew about the money and wanted it for himself.

'Does it say how much money it is in his letter?' asked Miss May.

Zhou shook her head. 'All I know is my boyfriend's friends were very excited about it. I think it must be quite a bit of money.'

'Do you have any idea what the marker looks like?' asked Barbie. Looking at Miss May and Patricia, she explained, 'It would be helpful to know just so we can be sure if we do find it.'

Zhou Li bit her lip in thought. 'You know, I think there might be an old one pinned to a board in the kitchen. One of the chefs likes to gamble, but is terrible at it and keeps the marker to remind himself how much debt he got into the last time he felt lucky.'

She dashed away to get it, returning less than a minute later with something in her right hand. It was a simple piece of card, not unlike the Luggage Legends tag they found. This one was cream instead of white and embossed on one side with a colourful lily and Chinese symbols going down one edge. On the bottom was a number – 053.

Barbie took it when Zhou offered.

Chelsea returned to the table, her phone call completed, just as Zhou's manager came looking for her. Getting berated by her manager in rapid-fire Chinese, Zhou apologised, left the ladies with both the original letter and her handwritten translation, and scurried away.

They caught Chelsea up quickly on what they had just learned.

'So what's our next move?' she asked, sucking up noodles fast so they could get back to searching for the truth.

Patricia said, 'Well, we now have a probable motive for Kris Wu's murder. Someone wanted the marker, but at this point we don't know if they got it or not.'

Miss May butted in. 'I think we should assume they did not. If the marker has already been cashed in, there wouldn't be so many people trying to find it.'

'True,' Patricia conceded. 'I think we can also assume Kris Wu's wife hasn't arrived yet.'

'Why's that?' asked Barbie.

'She didn't get to the letter. We got there first.'

'But she didn't have the token to exchange at Luggage Legends,' Chelsea pointed out. 'Surely that means even if she is here, she couldn't get to the briefcase.'

Patricia liked how sharp her new friends were.

'How was he going to get it to her?' asked Barbie. 'The letter was in case he died before she arrived. Hold on …' Barbie had her lips skewed to one side in a classic deep thought pose. 'Ignoring that I cannot see how she was ever going to get the card to collect the briefcase, what was the money for and where did it come from?'

Patricia's head snapped up, locking eyes with Miss May. They didn't realise they were both thinking the same thing until both blurted simultaneously, 'He stole it!'

'That's what Mr Yibo told us,' Barbie pointed out patiently.

She wasn't wrong but neither Miss May nor Patricia had believed him.

'He was lying,' Miss May insisted. 'But maybe there was some truth in the lie.'

'It was stolen …' Patricia tried to link her thoughts to arrive at a conclusion.

'But not from Mr Yibo,' concluded Miss May.

'Or not from the Fou Chin Clan,' added Patricia.

Barbie said, 'Wow. You two are good together.'

Chelsea frowned, maybe a little jealous that her aunt had found a such a good sleuthing partner, but went back to reading the letter.

Chelsea read through it twice while they ate, all four women fuelling themselves for whatever might come next. With a ticking clock and the lives of Petey and Bobbie on the line, sleep didn't seem like an option. They were going to have to keep going until they cracked the case.

Neither Miss May nor Patricia had said it yet, but they were both thinking the same thing. There was an obvious next move for them, and it involved a trip to see a loan shark called Freddie Lee.

As they were getting up, Chelsea tutted as she remembered something.

'I forgot to say, Teeny messaged me. She's on her way here and asked where we are staying.'

'Where are you staying?' asked Barbie.

Chelsea admitted, 'We didn't get that far yet. We figured we could sort that out later.'

It was getting late to find accommodation already.

'So where did you say to meet us?' asked Miss May.

Chelsea reached the door to the restaurant and pulled it open, letting the cool night air in. 'I said I'd get back to her. What's the address for the place we are going? I'll give her that.'

The Man with the Money

Approaching the area known as Chinatown, Patricia felt her pulse getting noticeably faster. They were attracting attention.

Unwanted attention. No one approached, but they spotted several men watching as they advanced up the street.

The address for the loan shark was in Kris Wu's letter, he clearly expected his wife to go there but she didn't have the marker. If they understood correctly, Kris Wu intended to place it in the briefcase with the letter but hadn't been able to. He might have been on his way to do it when he was killed, but whatever the case, the marker's location was unknown.

At 6152 Elizabeth Street they paused. It was the right address but the business to their front was a haberdashery.

'Why would a shop selling linen and thread be open at this time of the day?' wondered Miss May out loud. The question wasn't really a question. It was a prompt to make her companions answer.

'Because it's not really a linen and thread store. It's a front. Fancy front. A haberdashery. Is that what this is called?' replied Chelsea.

Patricia rubbed at an itch on the tip of her nose. This American girl really did babble when nervous. 'Yes. That would be my guess too.'

'In we go then.' Barbie started forward, angling toward the open front door. Her friends needed half a second to get their feet moving, and in the gap between Barbie setting off and the other three ladies following, a man the size of a bear stepped out of the Haberdashery's doorway.

He had to turn sideways to do it because his shoulders were wider than the door. He had a tattoo that covered more than one half of his face and a shaved head. At a guess, he had to weigh three-hundred and fifty pounds and most of it was muscle.

Barbie uttered something unprintable as her feet faltered.

Miss May was not so easily put off. 'Hello,' she waved to the giant man. 'We're here to see Freddie Lee. Is he in?'

The giant man's brow furrowed in a deep frown. 'Why do you want to see Mr Lee?' His voice was so deep it sounded like his tonsils had to be anchored to the bottom of the ocean. More than that though, his tone and demeanour were discouraging. He had told them to go away without actually saying the words.

Miss May's reply came smoothly. 'We know the location of the marker everyone is looking for.'

The giant's right eyebrow climbed his head, at which altitude it probably felt faint from lack of oxygen. If he had a reply for Miss May, they never got to hear it because a voice echoed out from within to change the situation.

'Let them in, Tommy.' The voice was older and nowhere near as deep, though it was distinctly male.

Tommy the giant stepped to one side, unblocking the door so the women could enter.

Barbie was the first to cross the threshold, her concern for her brother more powerful than the nerves she felt. However, once inside, she couldn't see where the voice might have originated from. There were two women in the shop, both in their late forties. They looked to be sisters and were silently working at one end, laying out long swathes of bright orange material.

The small sound of a foot moving through fine dust drew Barbie's eyes cross the room. Ducking her head slightly, she spotted a man with thinning grey hair sitting alone at a table against the far wall. He held a ledger in one hand and a pen in the other. His focus was entirely on the task before him.

As Barbie approached, her companions weaving through the shop behind her, the old man looked up, drew in a breath through his nose to then release it as a sigh before closing the ledger.

Swivelling in his chair so he faced them, he asked. 'Can I help you, ladies?'

Barbie was the first to speak. 'We are trying to work out who killed Kris Wu. My brother and his friend have been arrested for the crime, but they didn't do it. We think he might have been killed for the marker that you gave him. Who knew about it?' She didn't say please after her questions because she was on an emotional rollercoaster and being polite simply slipped her mind.

The man studied Barbie's face for several seconds before answering.

'What happened to Kris Wu was his own doing. He brought it entirely upon himself.'

'What does that mean?' Patricia wanted to know. 'Do you know who killed him?'

The Chinese man turned his head to look at her. 'I do not. Such things are not of interest to me. I manage this city's money, remaining neutral in all things and guaranteed protection because I can financially cripple any of the gangs with a line in my ledger. Kris Wu brought me money to hold much the same as anyone else would. Where it came from is also of no interest. However, if the rumours are true, it was not his.'

'Whose was it?' asked Miss May instantly, beating Patricia to the question by a split second.

Freddie Lee met her gaze. 'I neither know nor care and if I did know I would not tell you. If your friends are innocent of Kris Wu's murder their situation is regrettable. However, it is not one I can influence.'

'Did Kris Wu say when he was coming back for it?' Patricia posed a question she thought the man might answer.

The loan shark considered it for a second but chose to speak. 'I believe he hoped to return for it tomorrow. He acted as if there was an event due to occur and he needed somewhere safe for the money until then – twenty million dollars is a lot of money to carry around.'

'Twenty million!' gasped all four women as one voice.

Mr Lee didn't reply, he blinked once and waited for the ladies to ask another question.

'Please,' begged Barbie, tears beginning to brim as the hopelessness of their race against time got the better of her. 'Can you tell us anything that will help us to find Kris Wu's murderer?'

The man's attention shifted once again, but not to Barbie. Instead, he looked toward the door before shouting a single word. 'Tommy.'

The giant ducked back into the building, focusing his attention of the four women.

'The ladies are leaving, Tommy. Please show them out.'

Tommy began moving instantly, his legs controlled by Freddie Lee's words. The threat was unspoken but it was clear, nevertheless.

Barbie came forward, placing her hand on Freddie's left forearm as she begged him, 'Please. I need to help my brother. If you know who killed Kris Wu, please tell me. Or point us in the right direction if you cannot reveal the name.'

Tommy was just about to grab the back of Patricia's collar. He operated within a very simple set of rules – he did whatever Freddie Lee said and he did it fast and generally with a side order of violence.

Freddie raised his hand to make Tommy pause.

Miss May sensed a chink in the loan shark's armour. The young blonde woman had begged for his help and offered him a way to do it that would not break any codes. He wouldn't give a name, but perhaps he would give them a steer.

'Can you help us?' Miss May asked, her voice a firm but gentle whisper.

What none of the women knew was that Freddie Lee had no intention of helping them. He was, however, prepared to help himself.

The money he held for Kris Wu wasn't the kind of money he wanted. It was stolen for a start, and the people it was stolen from would know by now that he held it. Freddie was connected and respected and that meant the owners would examine their options before coming directly to him – such things caused territorial wars and backlash that always led to terrible bloodshed. However, despite what he told the women about being protected and his ability to cripple anyone should he choose to, there was too much money on the line for the owners to write it off, and sooner or later, they would choose to pay Freddie a visit.

It was with that in mind that he employed the women.

'Finding Kris Wu's killer will not resolve your problem,' he advised them, making each of the women frown in confusion. 'You claim to know the location of the marker. Retrieving it will remove any reason for the two men to be held in custody and eradicate the death mark they both carry.'

'What? How?' Barbie didn't understand at all. 'How will finding this stupid marker help my brother?'

Freddie nodded to Tommy again, who mimed taking his blackjack from his inner jacket pocket as a question to his boss. The small shake of Freddie's head went unnoticed by the ladies. So too the disappointed look on Tommy's face.

'It is time for you to leave, ladies. I wish you luck in your quest and advise you to not disturb me again unless you have the marker.'

As Tommy loomed, using his size to get the women moving since his boss didn't want them hurt, the four sleuths all hurried back across the fake haberdashery and out of the door.

Tommy followed them out, planting his enormous frame to block the entrance once again.

'Where to now?' asked Chelsea.

Miss May heard her question, but her attention was aimed down the street. So, too, was Patricia's, who had seen the exact same thing.

'Um, Chels. We may need to do that running thing again,' murmured Barbie, tracking Patricia's gaze.

Hatchet Men

'Who are they?' asked Barbie, doing her best to stop her voice from squeaking when she spoke.

Fifty yards down the street were a dozen men wearing matching suits and little black masks that covered their eyes – kinda like a masquerade ball accessory. They didn't look like they wanted to go dancing though. The dull black hatchets each man carried were just one clue.

A small Chinese woman wearing the same eye mask but dressed in an emerald-green winter coat and shiny black thigh-length boots with laces down the sides, appeared from behind them, striding through their midst until she was at the head.

'You are the women who know where the marker is.' It was a statement, not a question.

'We don't have it,' replied Miss May. 'We don't even really understand what it is.'

Patricia added, 'We are looking for it only so we can help our friends. They didn't kill Kris Wu. Was he part of your ... club?' Patricia hazarded. She suspected the right word was gang, but that sounded offensive in her head.

The Chinese woman blinked, her eyes never leaving the four women trapped in the street.

Barbie glanced to her left to discover Tommy, the man mountain that he was, had elected to retreat inside the haberdashery and close the door. He was inside now, looking out with the two older women who worked there standing either side of him.

Terrified again, and with fear powering her pulse, Barbie stammered. 'I just want to clear my brother's name. I don't care what happens to the marker or who gets it.'

'Ha!' spat the Chinese woman. 'You don't care about twenty million dollars stolen from the Shenyang gang? Whoever returns that money to the Shenyang will be accorded honour and territory. Kris Wu was foolish to believe he could escape with it. Hiding it with Freddie Lee was a mistake. He should have left when he had the chance. No one cares who killed him, the location of the marker is all that matters now.'

The woman, whoever she was, had given Miss May, Patricia, Barbie, and Chelsea more information in the last thirty seconds, than they had amassed so far tonight. Each was processing what they had just learned, rooted to the spot outside the haberdashery and certain the hatchet-toting, eye mask wearing, crazy Chinese gangsters facing them would give chase if they attempted to move.

Unfortunately, the Chinese woman believed the women had to know more than they were letting on and planned to be vigorous in extracting any information.

Bringing her right arm up to point down the street, she snarled, 'Get them.'

Her command elicited a banshee war cry from the six men spread out to her left. While those to her right remained in place, those to her left raised their hatchets and charged.

If the ladies needed any encouragement to get moving, they had it. With squeals of terror, they twisted through one hundred and eighty degrees and fled.

The end of the street where it met a busier road was no more than twenty yards away. Even towing Miss May along – Barbie and Chelsea had hold of her arms – they would make it that far before the gang caught them.

What then though?

It was a question for later. The only thing for right now, was to run and that was what they did.

Ahead, the cross street was quiet. Cars going back and forth which might have signified the chance of help or rescue were non-existent, so they hit the junction and ploughed straight on over it. There were headlights to their left, a single car rolling toward them but too far away to be of any help.

The gang were chasing, gaining fast. Barbie's phone was in her hand, desperately calling nine-one-one though she did not believe there was time for the call to even connect.

Fearing they would be caught at any second, the sound of an engine racing followed by cries of alarm and then pain made all four women glance over their shoulders.

The six pursuing Chinese men had all reached the cross street at the same time and though they should have all been able to cross the street long before the only car in the road got to them, they were somehow all flying through the air.

All six had been run down!

Behind them and screeching to a stop was a shiny black Buick LeSabre from the 1970's. It was a mammoth car and had ploughed through the small Chinese men like they were skittles.

As the women stared and their hearts refused to beat, the men rained back to the Earth like confetti.

Then Chelsea noticed the horrified looking driver and her eyes bugged out of her head. 'Teeny!'

Miss May gasped for breath, the sudden burst of energy demanding more oxygen than she had, but though her legs were protesting from all the running, she could see salvation and was ready to run again to get to it.

Teeny was their way out. All they had to do was get to the car, but Teeny was getting out, and back at the haberdashery, the remaining hatchet-wielding maniacs were coming her way fast.

'Teeny!' barked Miss May. 'Teeny, get back in the car!'

The six Chinese men were strewn across the road. Well, actually five of them were. One was lying across the hood of Teeny's car. He was trying to get up and still had hold of his hatchet.

'I didn't see them!' protested Teeny, her hands gripping either side of her face in horror. 'I saw you cross the road and accelerated to catch up. They came out of nowhere!'

Chelsea shouted, 'Teeny, get back in the car!'

Miss May was bringing up the rear, Chelsea still towing her along. They were going to get to the car but the remaining six men with their hatchets were running straight for the other side of Teeny's vehicle and it was going to be a close thing if the petite woman didn't get back behind the wheel really rather soon.

Barbie was running for the driver's door but changed her trajectory when the man lying on the hood pushed himself back to upright. There was blood coming from his mouth, and an angry sneer that showed his teeth when he lifted his hatchet and roared.

He was going to take a swipe at Teeny.

Barbie, athletic little minx that she is, drove off with her right foot and leapt into the air. She sailed across the hood to connect with the man's chest.

Teeny, facing the wrong way, hadn't even seen the man was there until he yelled his intention to kill her.

Patricia, next to arrive, wasted no time on introductions, throwing herself through the open driver's door to land behind the steering wheel.

In a mild state of shock and confused about what was happening, Teeny's eyes bugged clear out of her head.

'Help! Help, I'm being carjacked! Help!'

Barbie landed, following the man down and kicking the hatchet away before springing back to throw herself into the front passenger seat of the car.

Teeny shouted again. 'Waaaah! Carjackers!'

Miss May and Chelsea shouted back, 'Teeeennnnnyyyy! Get in the car!'

Patricia had the steering wheel in her hands and was poised to go, her eyes on the final two members of their team. The second they were in the car she was going to stamp on the pedal, and she wasn't going to stop until they were somewhere many miles away.

Chelsea dropped Miss May's arm to grab Teeny instead. Teeny was utterly bewildered by events and her feet were too confused to work out which way they should point. It proved arbitrary because Chelsea threw her into the back of the car, diving in after her and pulling her legs in to leave room for Miss May.

In an uncharacteristic display of excitement, Miss May screamed, 'Pedal to the metal, Patty!' as her feet left the tarmac and she landed on the backseat of the car a half second later. She expected to find herself slammed into the back of the seat as the car took off, but with the Chinese men now getting to their feet and their friends about to arrive, the car was going nowhere.

'Where's the gearstick?' wailed Patricia.

With no time to explain, Barbie jumped across the car, pushed the lever down one to engage drive and stamped her right foot down on top of Patricia's.

The car took off like a cat with a firecracker up its butt.

However, there were two women trying to steer it and the force of acceleration made it impossible for Barbie to get back into her seat.

All five women were screaming, and they were not the only ones, for in their haste to escape, they hit one of the injured men Teeny had already run over once and he was now clinging to the car's hood.

'There's a man on the bonnet!' shrieked Patricia.

From the back, Chelsea questioned, 'Bonnet? What the heck is a bonnet?'

'She means the hood!' yelled Barbie, trying to yank the wheel to throw the gangster off. She was turning it in the opposite direction to Patricia and consequently achieving nothing.

Half-buried under Chelsea as the younger woman tried to right herself and find her limbs, Teeny had nothing but questions.

'What in the name of sprinkles is going on?' she wanted to know. 'And who is this British lady?'

'Introductions later!' yelled Barbie, slapping Patricia's hand away and cranking the wheel hard to the left.

The car's back end slid out, threatening to escape Barbie's control, but the gangster lost his grip as the forces working against his body shifted. He fell from sight just as Barbie got the car pointing the right way again.

She let Patricia grab the wheel once more and after a quick check in the rear-view mirror, she slid back across to her own seat.

Miss May managed to shuffle her own butt around so it was in the seat. Now upright and feeling semi-safe, she posed a question, 'Teeny whose car is this and where is your car?'

'My car got a flat. Big Dan didn't have the right tire in his shop but said he could have one for me by tomorrow morning. When I told him I couldn't wait, he offered to loan me his uncle's car.'

'This is Big Dan's uncle's car?' questioned Chelsea. 'It looks like someone's pride and joy. It's immaculate.'

'Yeah,' Teeny blushed. 'I kinda had to twist his arm and promise to bring it back without a scratch on it. Do you think I might've dented the front fender when I ploughed into all those guys with hatchets? Who were they anyway?'

In the front of the car, Barbie tapped Patricia's arm. 'You can slow down now.'

They were still going at break-neck speed to get away, but no one was following.

Barbie twisted in her seat to check those in the back. 'We lost them,' she announced quietly. Extending her hand – awkward in the confined space - Barbie smiled at the newest member of the group. 'Hi, I'm Barbie.'

Teeny's confused response was drowned out by the 'Whooo!' sound of a police siren.

Still facing out the back of the car, her head blocking Patricia's rear-view, Barbie said, 'Uh-oh.'

Dirty Cop

'Uh-oh?' Chelsea said with a gulp, craning her own neck to see. 'Why uh-oh? Maybe some cops would be good right about now. Normally I wouldn't say that, but we could use a little reinforcement from a cop or two.'

Barbie sucked air between her teeth. 'Not this one.'

Patricia cruised to a stop wondering if she would get arrested, or just escorted to an airport and sent home. She had been speeding, driving erratically – which would probably make the officer think she was inebriated – didn't have a seat belt on, and it wasn't even her car. She couldn't even claim to have the owner's permission to drive it.

However, when she checked the driver's door mirror and saw who was getting out of the car, she doubted those concerns should be at the top of her list.

Lieutenant Danvers had his sidearm drawn and was approaching the car from the rear.

'What do we do, Patty?' Barbie chattered nervously, her eyes watching the seasoned cop as he neared their car. He was on the sidewalk, coming up on Patricia with his gun pointing down and both hands interlocked to control it.

Would he simply shoot them all? Just how dirty was he? Twenty million was a lot of motivation after all. Maybe he killed Kris Wu.

Coming alongside their windows, the five women in the car were silent. Nervously, Patricia powered down her window.

Danvers stared inside, his eyes narrowed, looking at each face in turn. Three seconds ticked by and just when Miss May was about ready to burst from the tension, the cop's shoulders sagged, and he swore.

'You teamed up then?' he concluded. 'And brought in another friend,' he added observing Teeny sandwiched in the back of the car. 'How are you all still alive? Are you all okay?'

His demeanour was throwing Patricia. Her left hand had been gripping the door handle, ready to throw it open and into his shins if the cop showed the slightest sign of raising his weapon. Now he was asking how they were? It was such an unexpected shift from what she expected, she felt it much akin to discovering her dogs could play the bagpipes.

Wrestling her eyebrows under control for they had made a bid for freedom via the top of her head, she was beaten to the punch by Miss May when from the backseat, she asked, 'Why didn't you call for backup in the alley?'

Lieutenant Danvers put his gun back into the holster inside his jacket and reached up to grab something out of sight on top of the car. A wrenching sound of metal on metal preceded his hands coming back into view with a hatchet in them.

'I guess you met the Tianjin gang. The hatchet is their calling card.'

Patricia chose to seek clarification, 'Eye masks, nice suits, generally murderous disposition?'

'That's them,' Danvers confirmed. 'Led by a nice lady called Vera Wong. She likes to kill people by cutting them into pieces.'

Barbie cringed. 'Ewwww.'

Miss May levered her door open. It was cramped in the back of the car, and she had a truckload of questions for the officer who was yet to answer her first one.

Hearing Miss May's door open, Barbie got out too, closely followed by Teeny and Chelsea. Finally, Patricia worked out how to put the car into 'park' and joined her friends on the sidewalk, though obviously she thought of it as a pavement.

Seeing the women leave the car, Danvers met Miss May's eyes. Her expression was expectant, and he supplied the answer she wanted.

'I couldn't call for backup, it would have tipped off the person I am trying to catch.'

'And who is that?' Miss May demanded.

Barbie held up her hand, saying, 'Wait. The man you are trying to catch? As in catch for the murder of Kris Wu?'

Lieutenant Danvers had the decency to look guilty. 'Maybe.' Seeing that he was about to get hit with a stack of questions, he followed up quickly with, 'Look, I don't know. Okay? You're about to ask if I think Bobbie and Petey did it, and the answer is no, okay?' He had to raise his voice and plough on to stop the barrage of questions coming from the five women. 'I had to lock them up. The beat cops arrested them, and I knew if I let them out, the gangs would have picked them up five minutes later.'

The five women formed an imposing line a yard in front of his face, their glares forcing him to take a step backward.

Patricia growled. 'I think you've got some explaining to do, Lieutenant.'

Danvers wanted to go somewhere safer, to get the women off the street, but they could feel the opportunity to find out the truth and after his revelation about knowing the boys were innocent, they were going nowhere until they heard everything.

'Okay,' he relented when it was clear they were not going to give up and wouldn't be moved. 'Kris Wu is ... was a confidential informant – a CI - a person who reports to law enforcement on criminal activity. Most usually, these people are operating on the wrong side of the law and that was certainly true of Kris Wu.'

'How did you recruit him?' asked Miss May.

Danvers gave a tired laugh. 'I didn't. He wasn't my CI,' he explained though it added little clarity. 'He was CI for an FBI agent called Hu Chang. I was assigned by my chief to be Hu's local liaison officer. We've been working together ever since the Alliance of Families was exposed.' He looked at Patricia and Barbie. 'I believe I have you to thank for that.'

Patricia hated being praised. Hated it. She inclined her head to show thanks and left it at that.

Danvers continued, 'Agent Chang was sent to crack the new gangs taking over in New York. They were quick to jump on the opportunities up for grabs with the loss of the major organised crime families. There had been a power struggle and the gangs are still sorting out where the new territory lines are. The Shenyang are the biggest but there are other major players. Kris Wu just got married a short while ago – he met a woman on a trip to China last year. The point is, he wanted out and Hu Chang was able to recruit him. Kris Wu would get immunity for his crimes if he helped us take down the new gangs before they could establish their power base. New York is always going to be a hotspot – a lot of drugs come in through the ports and the gangs control its distribution. Then there is protection, prostitution ...'

Miss May butted in, 'You can skip that part. We all know what gangs get up to.'

'I don't,' said Teeny. 'I'm interested. Are the hatchets part of the protection or the prostitution?'

'No time,' Chelsea pointed out. 'We need to focus on Petey.'

'Anyway,' Danvers tried to steer the women back onto topic. 'Agent Chang vanished two days ago, and I think he was killed. I tried to contact Kris Wu, but he had gone to ground. Then, yesterday I started hearing all these rumours that someone had ripped off the Shenyang gang. Before I know it, Kris Wu gets stabbed in an alleyway and dies. He was miles from his turf. I'm trying to work out what was going on, but I think he took the money and was planning to run with it.'

Patricia interrupted him, 'He gave it to Freddie Lee.'

'The loan shark?' blurted Lieutenant Danvers, his jaw dropping open. Then he tipped his head back and closed his eyes. 'Of course. That's why there are people out looking for a missing marker. He dropped the money off with Freddie Lee. The Shenyang will try to resolve this without bloodshed – killing Freddie would be bad for business; he manages the finances of half the gangs in this city. It's also why everyone wants the marker. They can claim the money and try to vanish with it. If they get away, they are rich. Or they can hand it back to the Shenyang because everyone assumes they are going to be the ones to take over the city's criminal empire. Having the Shenyang owe you a debt would put a person in a strong position.'

'Why would anyone want that?' asked Teeny, still trying to catch up on all that had happened.

Lieutenant Danvers looked down at her face. 'Imagine having a deadly gang you could call upon to do you a favour when someone ticked you off?'

Teeny pursed her lips. 'Yeah, I can see how that might come in handy. I'd like to stop Big Dan's ex-girlfriend from calling him and asking for "car repairs". I mean, her car did break down, but come on, lady.'

Danvers went on. 'For the smaller gangs, it could be a ticket to the big time, but whatever the case, there are a lot of people looking for the marker. The question is, why did Kris Wu take the money?'

'His wife is about to arrive from China with his daughter,' said Barbie. 'We found a letter from him to his wife explaining it all.'

Danvers choked out a surprised gasp. 'Wow. You ladies sure don't hang around.'

Unnoticed by the small group, a panel van was approaching. It was dark grey to blend into the background and the windows were tinted almost completely black to hide the occupants. Traffic was going by steadily, so a van passing them was nothing unusual. However, as it neared the parked car and the gaggle of women on the sidewalk, the side door slid open.

This went unnoticed by the five women; they were all facing the other way, but Lieutenant Danvers saw it.

A Secret No One Knows

Lieutenant Danvers bellowed, 'Down!' and threw himself forward. As he reached for his gun a man appeared in the side door of the panel van, hanging on to the top handle.

Danvers saw a flash as the gun started spewing bullets long before he could bring his own weapon into play. He barged into Barbie, knocking her down as he tried to get his body between the civilians and the shooter.

Falling backward, Barbie heard the zip-crack of bullets going over her head. With panicked eyes, she checked left and right, to see her friends hunkering down to the sidewalk. The van could be heard accelerating down the street, its wheels burning rubber to escape the scene.

In an instant, the street was quiet again. Quiet except for the sound of Danvers' laboured breathing and the tinkling noise of small glass fragments falling to the asphalt.

The lieutenant had some choice words to say. So did Teeny, who was staring in rapt horror at the three missing side windows on Big Dan's uncle's beautiful vintage Buick.

Acting with uncharacteristic poise, Chelsea already had her hands on the wound at the top righthand side of the cop's chest. The bullets had been fired erratically from a moving vehicle, most of them striking the car or the wall behind, but two hit Lieutenant Danvers when he failed to heed his own advice and duck. Neither wound looked life threatening, but the one in his chest was still inside and would require surgery to remove.

Gritting his teeth as he levered himself off the ground with Barbie and Chelsea helping him, Danvers used his radio to report 'officer down'. With that done, he turned his attention to the women.

'I told you not to investigate this,' he growled.

Patricia, feeling sympathetic toward the officer now that she knew he wasn't dirty and had probably just saved their lives, said, 'We had no choice. You could have told us Bobbie and Petey were innocent.'

'What do we do now?' asked Teeny. 'They don't have to go to the clanker, right? They get outta jail free, like in Monopoly?'

Danvers shot her a look. 'Goodness no. I charged them with murder. The only other person who knows they are innocent is my chief. Without him changing things, they will be transferred to state pen in the morning. Like I said, if they get released the gangs will pick them up. It would be like signing their death sentence.' He was starting to look a little pale.

'But they don't know anything,' wailed Barbie.

'But the gangs don't know that,' Danvers pointed out. 'They had already been arrested by the time I got involved. It was too late to undo it. Look, worst case scenario they do a couple of days in state pen. Yes, it's not a nice place, but they will be safe there.'

'Safe!' blurted Miss May. 'The Fou Chin Clan already promised to kill them both the moment they arrive if we don't find the marker and hand it over.'

Danvers clearly hadn't thought of that. 'Really?' He swore, colouring the air a little more with his choice of words. 'I need to speak to my chief.' Danvers' eyes dropped, and he mumbled his next words.

'Hey, stay with us,' demanded Barbie, gripping the man's shoulder hard to jolt him back to life before he lost consciousness. 'It's better if you stay awake.'

She could see how much blood he had lost, they all could.

Remembering his train of thought, he managed to say, 'We need to hold them at the station.'

The sound of distant sirens was coming closer, the cavalry on their way to save one of their own. Seconds later, a police car screeched around a distant corner and into sight, the wheels gripping the road's surface as the driver controlled the skid. A second car followed close behind and an aid car was right behind it.

The sight drew the attention of the ladies for a few seconds and when they looked back down at the stricken cop, he was unconscious.

The paramedics gave aid and were swift to assess his need to be evacuated to hospital as a vital emergency. What had not initially looked like life-threatening wounds, were in fact exactly that. He was bleeding out, and though the paramedics were confident he would survive, they nevertheless acted as though they were in a race against the clock to keep him alive.

His departure left the five women on the sidewalk with the cops. They wanted statements but were surprised by what the women had to say now that Lieutenant Danvers was being treated. It all got too complicated for the officers to decipher so they had them follow them back to their precinct where they hoped to sort it out.

All five women hoped this was it. They were going to get to speak to Danvers' chief and he would have sufficient pull to have the boys released. Or, if not released, then at least held at the station until someone could corroborate what they were saying.

It took over an hour of increasingly irritated sitting on the uncomfortable plastic chairs for the chief to finally summon them, but then they discovered it wasn't the chief they were going to see at all.

'Hi, I'm Captain Mainwaring,' a haggard looking man in a cheap suit hung through the doorframe into reception. 'I was told you ladies had a story to tell me.' He had a coffee stain across his shirt and tie.

Barbie was the first to her feet, but the others all followed suit. Their reaction made the captain's eyebrows rise and he made a down motion with one hand.

'This doesn't need all five of you. I'm sure one or two will do. Follow me.'

The women turned inward, looking at each other.

Barbie said, 'You go, Patty. Make him listen, please.' There was heart-breaking need in Barbie's voice. She wanted this to be over for her brother.

'And you, Miss May,' Teeny volunteered her friend. Miss May was the best choice for their group – she was the least likely to lose her cool and everyone knew it.

The two older women looked inward at each other, nodded silently, and followed the captain, not that he had bothered to wait for them. It was a simple task – tell the senior cop what they knew, make sure Bobbie and Petey were safe, and then walk away. They didn't need to solve this case. It didn't matter about the stolen money and the missing marker.

Their sole focus was the two innocent young men.

They turned a corner in the narrow corridor behind the station's front reception desk and found the captain waiting for them and looking impatient.

'Come on, ladies. I have too many things on my plate already. Let's get this done.' He didn't hold the door and didn't ask them to sit or offer them a drink. He did, however, take a call when the women got into his office which made them wait another minute while he barked orders at someone.

When he dropped the phone back into its cradle – the office and its furnishings really were that old - he gave them a semi-interested expression.

'Now, I believe you have evidence that the two men I have in custody for the murder of Kris Wu are innocent, yes?'

'Where is the chief?' asked Patricia, concerned that this was not going the way she expected.

'He had a heart attack at six o'clock this evening. You've got me instead. I'm the stand-in chief. So, what evidence?'

A heart attack? Danvers said the chief was the only one at the station who knew what was going on!

'The two men are innocent. They need to be released,' blurted Patricia.

Captain Mainwaring waited for the punchline.

Miss May tried to explain. 'Lieutenant Danvers only charged them so they wouldn't be released. He wanted to protect them from the Chinese gangs who are chasing a marker worth twenty million dollars.'

'Is that what they killed Kris Wu for?' the captain asked.

'They didn't kill him,' Patricia protested. 'The chief knew about it. Can we speak to him? Did he ... die?

'Die? No. But he is in surgery. Emergency triple bypass apparently. He needs to get back quickly because doing his job is going to kill me. No wonder he had a heart attack.'

'Please,' begged Miss May. 'You're not hearing us. The situation is urgent. Desperate. Time sensitive. Should I keep going?' She got a glare in response but powered onward. 'Lieutenant Danvers knows the boys are innocent. So does your chief. Danvers said they were the only two in the loop. It has something to do with an FBI agent called Hu Chang. He went missing two days ago and Lieutenant Danvers thinks one of the Chinese gangs found out about who he was and killed him. Kris Wu was Agent Chang's CI. Chang was killed and Wu took the money and tried to run. He had to stick around though, because his wife and daughter are on their way here, so he placed it with a loan shark called Freddie Lee. Danvers thinks Kris Wu was killed for the marker, but the marker's missing and no one seems to know who took it. That's why half of Chinatown is looking for it. You need to stop Bobbie and Petey from being transferred to the state penitentiary in the morning or they'll be killed by the Chinese gangs when they get there. Can you do that for us?'

Miss May fell silent, her story told. She and Patricia waited for the captain to speak.

He swung his eyes from one to the other and then back to the first again.

'I'm not hearing any evidence,' he pointed out. 'Do you have any?'

Patricia pulled out the letter they found in the briefcase. 'This is a letter Kris Wu wrote to his wife. It's in Chinese but we had it translated.'

The captain took it, inspected it for about five seconds and put it down on his desk next to a coffee spill.

'I'll have someone look into it, okay?' Seeing their faces, he repeated himself with a little added hardness in his voice. 'Okay? I'm stand in chief, one of my senior detectives got shot tonight in a drive by shooting that might have tie-ins to Chinese gang operations and I'm not making any decisions about anything until I know for certain it won't cost me my pension.'

The man was clearly feeling harassed, and though both Patricia and Miss May were unhappy with their result, they could see they were not going to do any better.

The captain shouted for an officer to escort the ladies back to their friends in reception and was on the phone before a young man in uniform appeared.

It wasn't exactly a bust, but it was far from a result. Mercifully, Patricia had an inkling of a plan forming at the back of her head. This was not the first time she had faced similar odds. There were rival gangs all after one thing and they believed she, or her friends, held the key to getting it.

Her plan was nuts, but it had worked once before. Sort of.

Rugged Tires

'No, Patty!' exclaimed Barbie. 'Patty, that is a terrible idea.'

'Do you have a better one?' Patricia countered knowing that her blonde friend was going to have to say no.

'Hold on. Just, quick clarification,' Chelsea said. 'What exactly is "doing a Malta"?'

Barbie frowned at her English friend. 'Malta is a place we went to a few months ago. Patricia found herself in possession of a data storage device that half the spies on the planet were ready to kill for. I'm still not sure how we got out of that one alive.'

'We did it by turning everyone against themselves,' Patricia reminded her. 'Everyone wants the marker. If we let them know we have it, we can lure them all to a single point and have the cops arrest them all.'

Miss May flared her eyes. 'That's a bold plan, Patricia.'

Barbie rolled her eyes. 'Patty specialises in those. Once we all dressed up as corpses and pretended to be zombies to scare people out of the infirmary on the ship.'

Patricia snorted a laugh. 'Yeah, that was a good one.' Catching Barbie's expression, she pointed out, 'Hey, it worked, didn't it?'

Teeny voiced her opinion. 'It sounds kinda dangerous. Not that I'm afraid or anything. Just an observation, like, oh the sky is blue, that plan sounds reckless and terrifying.'

'It is,' agreed Barbie.

Patricia raised her hands in surrender. 'Ok. No pulling a Malta. I get it. Let's come up with something else.'

'All we need is something tangible to take to the cops, right?' Chelsea got everyone to listen to her. 'We need ice-cold, rock-hard evidence that will cast doubt on Bobbie and Petey's guilt.'

'Yeah,' agreed Teeny. 'Do we have anything like that?'

Miss May shook her head. 'Nope.'

'How about if we find the marker?' asked Teeny.

Chelsea chuckled sadly. 'I mean, that would be great. Only problem? We don't have any idea where it is. Half of Chinatown is looking for it.'

'Actually,' started Patricia, the back of her head itching like mad as thoughts aligned in her head.

Miss May jumped in. 'I think maybe we do know where it is.'

She locked eyes with Patricia and they both blurted, 'The biker bar!'

'What?' questioned Barbie.

'Why would it be there?' Chelsea asked. 'I mean, a dive bar filled with drunk bikers ... seems like a questionable place to stash your millions.'

Teeny raised her hand. 'What biker bar?'

They explained on the way, filling Teeny in on more of the events she had missed that day.

Patricia explained what she heard as they were being kicked out of the bar. 'One of the men drinking in the bar complained about there being a Chinese guy in there the previous evening. I tried to question it at the time, but the owner kicked us out.'

Barbie was used to Patricia making massive leaps in her investigations and that they often turned out to be bang on the money, but this was a little too random even for her.

'A Chinese man was in the bar, Patty? How many Chinese men do you think live in New York?'

Miss May corrected her. 'The man didn't just say a Chinese man, he said a Chinese man came in, stayed a while and then left. Then another Chinese man arrived. First one and then another and then more.'

Chelsea was with Barbie. 'So? Barbie is right, there are lots of Chinese people in New York. How can you be so sure any of them were Kris Wu and why would that mean the marker is there?'

Miss May and Patricia exchanged a look, the English sleuth giving her American counterpart the nod so she could explain.

'The first man was Kris Wu.' Seeing confused faces looking back at her in the tight confines of Big Dan's car, she went back a step further. 'What do we know about Kris Wu?' she asked.

'Not much,' replied Chelsea.

'But what we do know is pertinent,' Miss May countered. 'He was a member of an organised crime family and had turned informant. He was providing information to an FBI agent, right?'

Barbie made a connection. 'He got spooked when the FBI agent was killed and worried they might be coming for him next.'

'Like maybe the guy gave up his name when they were "making him talk",' Teeny used air quotes around the terrifying term.

'Exactly,' agreed Miss May. 'Kris Wu is scared but he can't leave because his wife and child are about to arrive. Believing he has no choice but to run, he snatches a load of money, which he'll need to evade the gangs and start a new life somewhere else.'

Patricia took over the story, 'But he doesn't get away clean. Something he did, whether it was getting spotted by someone, or just that Agent Chang really did give up his name, they are on to him and so he leaves the letter for his wife.'

'Hold up,' Chelsea jumped in, seeing a flaw in their theory. 'How was his wife ever going to find the briefcase? We had the ticket for the luggage place. It was in the alley where he died. She had no way of tracking it down.'

Miss May tapped her nose with her pointer finger. 'Great question, Chels. My guess is that Mr Wu was trying to get to somewhere, but he never made it. His killer caught up to him before he could hand the letter over. I think he was on his way to Grand Central to drop off the marker with the letter and that was when his luck ran out.'

Barbie and Chelsea were still arguing. 'But if the killer caught up to him in the biker bar, how was it that he was in the same bar as Bobbie and Petey? That had to be after he left the biker bar, because he was killed after he left the Orange Banana Bar.'

Again, and quite frustratingly, Patricia and Miss May nodded.

With a hand, Miss May deferred to Patricia so she could explain.

Patricia pursed her lips and framed her thoughts before she started talking.

'If we go back to what the man said in Rugged Tires Biker Bar before we left, you will remember a Chinese man came in and then another, and then a whole group. The first was Kris Wu. He knew he was being tailed, so attempted to find somewhere he could hide out. If the gangs were looking for him, they might have positioned people at the Metro stations or in the streets.'

Chelsea picked up what the English woman was saying. 'He had to get off the streets and go somewhere the gangs might not look. Okay, okay. That makes sense.'

Patricia nodded. 'Hence a biker bar. He left the marker there somewhere, stayed for one drink and then tried to move on. Then his killer arrived. He was looking for Kris Wu because he wanted the marker. The killer planned to cash it in or hand it back to the Shenyang. Whichever it is doesn't matter, but he also left the bar when he discovered Kris Wu wasn't there and moved on. Kris Wu's aim must have been to get to Grand Central but the streets were crawling with Chinese gang members. He can't move for fear of being seen, so he ducks into yet another bar.'

'The Orange Banana,' guessed Teeny, smiling to herself for getting it right when Miss May nodded. 'That reminds me of the knock-knock joke, how does it go? Banana, banana, banana, orange ya glad I didn't say banana? Sorry. Bad time for a joke. Continue.'

'It's there that his killer finds him,' Miss May explained. 'Not sure how, but I'm assuming this killer was smart and has eyes everywhere. The point is, Kris Wu sees him and flees, probably going out of a back door which leads him into the alley where his luck truly runs out.'

Barbie finished the tale, 'Then Bobbie and Petey leave the bar, stop in the alley, and find Kris Wu bleeding to death and beyond saving.'

Chelsea frowned deeply, aiming her eyes at Patricia, 'How can you be so sure the marker is in the biker bar?'

Patricia shrugged. 'I'm not sure.'

Chelsea threw her hands in the air.

'But,' Miss May added quickly, 'we know Kris Wu went to see Freddie. We know Kris stole the money earlier that day, and we know the marker is yet to be found. The police would have been all over the Orange Banana Bar. I'm willing to bet we were sitting a few feet from it in Rugged Tires earlier today.'

The ladies fell silent, each holding their own thoughts as they covered the final couple of blocks back to the biker bar.

Barbie pulled out the old marker they picked up in the Chinese restaurant, turning it over and over in her hand and wondering what story it might hold.

Parking Big Dan's uncle's now battered vintage Buick around the corner from the Rugged Tires bar, the ladies paused for a second to discuss their strategy.

'What are we waiting for?' asked Teeny. Trapped in the middle of the backseat between Patricia and Miss May, she couldn't reach a door handle and had no idea why no one was moving.

'The owner told us not to come back,' explained Miss May. 'He wasn't pleased about the Chinese gangsters showing up in his bar.'

'Well, that's true,' agreed Chelsea. 'Except I saw the way the motorcycle club leader was looking at Miss Tall and Blonde,' she pointed out while trying to keep her tone neutral – she wasn't jealous of the younger, prettier, taller woman with the gravity defying chest. Not one bit, and you cannot prove otherwise.

Barbie's eyes took on a wistful look. 'Yeah, he was …'

'… shockingly good-looking?' Chelsea supplied. 'Like a giant bowl of ice cream you want to pour toffee sauce all over and eat with a spoon?'

'And sprinkles,' Teeny added. 'I mean, I didn't see the guy, but sprinkles never hurt.'

'I have a boyfriend,' Barbie protested. 'It's quite serious.'

Chelsea wasn't convinced. 'I have a boyfriend too. The guy in the biker bar was something else though.'

Interrupting the conversation for fear they might start discussing what they wanted to do to the biker man, Miss May said, 'Well, I don't like the idea of sending Barbie in alone with all those men.' She grabbed her door handle. 'Maybe the bar staff will have switched over and they won't know us,' she added hopefully.

'I mean, based on my limited knowledge of bar shifts, that seems pretty improbable,' chuckled Chelsea. 'It's only been a few hours. Sorry. Was that know-it-all-y?'

That so little time had passed, and they had squeezed so much drama into it seemed unfathomable, but the clock wasn't lying, it was only just ten o'clock.

'So, we're all going?' Teeny wanted to confirm, poised on the back seat and ready to get out. 'I've never been in a biker bar. I mean, I've been in bars, and there were bikers there. But, a real NYC biker bar? Kind of exciting.'

Patricia leaned forward to tap Barbie on the arm. 'We need to sex you up a bit, doll.'

Barbie huffed out a breath that ruffled her lips. 'Do I at least get to keep my clothes on this time?'

Wolf

By common vote, Barbie was to be used to distract the predominantly male clientele outside of the bar. The five women had spent five minutes adjusting Barbie's dress so it showed the maximum amount of cleavage, and rooting around in their various handbags and pockets to find some suitable makeup.

They also refused to return her coat once they got it off to sort out her dress.

'It gives you a vulnerable look,' Patricia did her best to convince her friend being cold was a small sacrifice.

'Plus, it um, highlights, certain uh, features you've got that might catch a man's eye. Or… poke it out,' added Chelsea, trying not to stare at Barbie's visible nipples.

Barbie glanced downward, and grimacing, she placed her hands over her boobs to warm them up.

'My dress is ruined, you know,' Barbie complained.

'It adds to the vulnerable look,' Patricia gave her a big thumbs up.

Accepting defeat, Barbie snatched the dusty blue mascara Patricia found in her handbag. Then she quickly tidied her hair using her reflection in the car's one remaining side window, and they found a fire engine red lipstick in the glove box.

'What is Big Dan's uncle doing with a red lipstick in his glovebox?' Chelsea asked and then decided she probably didn't want to know.

From the trunk, which Patricia confusingly called the boot, Teeny produced a pair of pink leather cowboy boots she'd hurriedly thrown in as she packed to leave Pine Grove. They didn't exactly go with Barbie's dress which had seen better days admittedly, but they were better than the sneakers she'd bought earlier.

'They're a bit tight,' winced the tall blonde as she forced her feet into the boots. Standing up, the women agreed that it didn't matter if she couldn't walk, the men outside the bar were going to struggle to notice anything other than her chest.

Out the front of Rugged Tires, there were now three times as many bikes parked. Chelsea tried to count them as she peered around the corner but gave up because people kept walking in front of them and new ones were still arriving.

'There're a lot of people in there now,' she summarised. 'I lost count at too many to karate kick by myself.'

Patricia grabbed hold of Barbie's arm. 'Are you okay with the plan, sweetie?'

Barbie understood the plan and was willing to go along with it because she wanted to save her brother. Being okay with it was a whole different thing.

She drew in a deep breath to steady her nerves and recited how they hoped it was all going to go.

'I parade around outside the bar, flirting with the men and drawing as many outside as I can.'

'How are you going to do that?' Teeny wanted to know.

Barbie sighed. 'I have a plan. You don't need to know what it is. I keep them entertained until you call me to say you have the marker and hope you come to rescue me in the car before I find myself kidnapped and on my way to some biker hideout in the countryside. Is that about right?' she asked with a distinct trace of snark in her voice.

Chelsea was feeling very much glad she wasn't the tall, pretty one in this particular moment. Not that she was ever going to be the tall one, unless she was standing next to Teeny and a bunch of toddlers.

With a final exhalation of air, Barbie lifted her head, jiggled her boobs around to make them sit higher and strolled around the corner. As she headed toward the bikers, Miss May, Patricia, Chelsea, and Teeny all hustled the other way, back around to the rear door where they knew the emergency exit could be accessed.

This time when they went inside, the owner wasn't there to surprise them. Passing the storeroom in the back as they made their way past the restrooms and toward the bar, they could hear a crowd outside the bar.

Squinting to get a view through the windows, they could see a wall of men out front, but no sign of Barbie.

'Do you think she'll be okay?' asked Miss May.

'Probably,' replied Patricia, somewhat hesitantly. 'However, the longer we leave her out there, the less likely it is that she remains that way.'

With that in mind, the ladies sidled into the bar area looking to see who was still there. The answer, incredibly, was no one. Looking into the bar from the back corner, they could see over a hundred people outside. Just inside the door, the two barmen and the owner were crammed together to get a look at the show outside without having to abandon the premises.

As silently as they could, the women split up to search.

For two seconds.

That was all it took to find the marker. Above the bar and along the walls, beer mats, foreign currency, and photographs were stapled. They were everywhere. There had to be a few thousand of them and many were faded with age and had to have been in the same place for years.

That Miss May spotted it the moment she stared at the first piece of wall was entirely typical of her. Chelsea often marvelled at how she seemed to see everything.

She picked out the thumb tack pinning it to the woodwork, held it aloft for the others to see, and started back toward the emergency exit.

Outside in the street, Barbie was beginning to get nervous. Her ploy, very simply, was to get all the men looking her way. With her body that wasn't hard to do, and she was prepared, if necessary, to drop the front of her dress and show off the goods. They were just a bunch of strangers – at least that's what she told herself – and she would never have to see them again. If she succeeded in saving her brother, it was no big deal.

What she hadn't counted on was the bikers having girlfriends with them.

Half a dozen ladies wearing thick denim or leather were advancing on her as she started to back away. They had a wide range of names they wished to call her, and they all fell into the same category.

Alone and starting to worry she might have to make a run for it in the too-tight pink cowboy boots, Barbie glanced left and right as she weighed up her options.

'Stop,' commanded a man's deep voice. It sounded like it was used to being obeyed, so it came as no surprise, and a blessed relief to Barbie, when the six women advancing on her with menacing expressions all stopped moving.

Their faces didn't change, but they did wait for further instruction.

'This lady is just looking to have a good time,' said the deep voice. The crowd of men outside the bar parted as the broad-shouldered, handsome man stepped out from between them. It was the same alpha male Barbie saw across the bar earlier. 'One cannot blame her for seeking out the real men of this city.'

The lady bikers retreated inside the bar, dragging some of the men with them.

'You look cold,' observed the alpha male, shrugging off his jacket and leather doublet. 'I have to keep my cut,' he said, taking back the leather waistcoat thing, 'but you can have my jacket.'

Barbie gratefully accepted it, revelling in the warm, masculine scent it gave off as she slipped it over her shoulders. It was big on her and that allowed her to wrap it around and overlap at the front. She was instantly warmer.

'Barbie, let's go!' shouted Chelsea. The women had arrived back at the corner of the building. Unsure what they might see, Chelsea stuck her head out to sneak a peek and was genuinely disappointed to find the tall blonde being romanced by the unfairly handsome biker.

'Barbie, is it?' the alpha male asked, his tone soothing and gentle. 'You look like you have had a tough day. Is there anything I can help you with?'

Finding her voice finally, Barbie said, 'I saw you in the bar earlier.'

'And I saw you,' he replied. 'The Chinese gang, have they continued to cause you bother?'

'A little,' Barbie admitted.

'Barbie! Come on!' yelled Patricia. 'We've got it. Let's go!'

'I have to go,' Barbie whispered, entranced by the pack leader's beguiling smile and eyes.

'Yes,' he nodded, 'Your friends appear impatient. Before you go.' He grabbed Barbie's left wrist, gently stopping her from escaping while he fished in his pocket for something.

At the corner, the women all saw the man grab their friend. As one they tensed, ready to go to her aid if that was what they had to do.

'He's going for a knife!' squealed Patricia.

What appeared in the man's hand a moment later wasn't a knife though, it was a pen. He bit the cap off, and holding Barbie's arm, he began inscribing his number. He finished it with his name 'Wolf' and brought his eyes back up to meet the blonde's.

'So you can give me back my jacket,' he explained. 'Call me when you are done.'

Mesmerised, Barbie had to really think about how her legs worked just to get them moving again.

Wolf pushed her away, releasing her wrist with a final word, 'Go.'

'Barbie! Hurry!' yelled Chelsea again with Teeny and Patricia making urgent gestures to break her reverie.

Coming to her senses, and wondering what had just happened, Barbie ran to the corner where her friends were waiting. Before she turned down the alley to head back to their car, she took one last look over her shoulder to find the bike pack leader still in the street, his muscular frame outlined by the streetlight behind him. Then, yanked by her arm, she lost sight of him.

They were on their way to Freddie Lee's but if they thought the worst of the evening was now behind them, they were very much mistaken.

New Player

'Hello, girls,' said a shadow just as they all got back to the Buick. A dark form detached itself from the side of a building in shadow to step into the light holding a machine pistol in its right hand. The man, unsurprisingly Chinese, was grinning as if he'd just been told something funny.

They were trapped again. Having parked out of the way to sneak into the bar via the back door, they were out of sight of everyone and all alone with an armed man. He wasn't wearing a suit and an eye mask, so he wasn't one of Vera Wong's men, and he wasn't displaying the symbol of Yibo's Fou Chin Clan. However, since there were so many other gangs and individuals after the marker, it did not come as a surprise that someone had found them.

'I believe you have something that belongs to me,' the man said, his voice calm and controlled.

'Who are you?' asked Miss May, attempting to keep her own voice calm.

The muzzle of the gun rose an inch. 'I'm not going to ask again,' the man growled. 'I already killed Kris Wu. I won't even break a sweat killing the five of you.'

'You killed Kris Wu!' blurted Barbie. 'You're the reason my brother is in jail!'

Patricia took a fast step forward to grab Barbie's arm before she did anything foolish.

Miss May asked, 'What makes you think we have the marker?'

The gunman chuckled. 'It was in that biker bar, wasn't it? I knew Kris had to have ditched it somewhere along the route. He knew he was going to get caught but even facing death, he couldn't give up the money. He must have told himself there was still a chance he could escape, and he would double back later to get the marker. Kris was so dumb. He fell for every lie I ever told him.'

The back of Patricia's skull itched; a sure sign that she was adding things up in her head and getting them right.

Barbie cried, 'My brother is in jail for your crimes.' She wanted to knock the gun from his hand and overpower him. She didn't know if she had the strength or the skill, but she certainly had the righteous energy.

The gunman shrugged. 'I don't care. Three seconds ladies. After that I shoot you full of holes and take the marker from your bodies.'

A second of silence ticked by.

'Here,' said Miss May, holding up the marker.

The gunman's eyes sparkled upon seeing it.

Barbie turned away from him, reaching out to take the small piece of embossed card from Miss May.

'I'll give it to him.'

Close enough to whisper, Chelsea blurted, 'That's our only bargaining chip. Once he has it, he's just gonna shoot us all. To death.'

Barely able to believe she was saying it, Barbie replied, 'When I hand it over, I'm going for his gun. He won't expect it. Be ready to back me up, okay? All we have to do is get him to the ground and call the police.' Barbie knew she was strong for a woman, her life as a gym instructor ensured her muscles were far more capable than they looked, and her friend, Patricia's butler, Jermaine, had taught her some simple fighting moves.

The man was Kris Wu's killer. If she could just get his gun, this nightmare would be over, and her brother would walk free.

'I'm coming with you,' whispered Chelsea.

When Barbie met Chelsea's eyes, Miss May hissed, 'She knows karate.'

Barbie just nodded. Unable to say anything else, she took the marker from Miss May's unresisting hand and turned around to face the gunman. She was going to distract him with the thing he wanted and put all her effort into taking the gun out of his hand. She could see the moves in her head. Grab his arm and force it down, spin into him with her left elbow high to connect with his face, then use both hands to twist his gun hand backward.

Chelsea could see it all too. Barbie was ahead of her, and she couldn't now nudge her to one side without their actions looking questionable. She would wait for Barbie to go for the gun then strike out at his hand.

Yeah, none of that happened.

The Sting

As Barbie took her first step toward the gunman, headlights swung into the alley to blind them all. Momentarily startled by the unexpected change in circumstances, Barbie should have grasped that moment to go for the gun.

Instead, she hesitated like any normal person would and missed her chance.

The gunman slammed into her, snatched the marker from her hand, and shoved her roughly away. As she fell back, she got to see the vicious leer on his face as he gripped the treasured piece of card triumphantly. Then the world filled with bright light and noise as he started firing, emptying a full magazine at the car heading his way.

Gunfire returned, the five women hugging the dirty asphalt as shots whizzed by above their heads. It shut off almost instantly as the sound of fast feet reached the next corner and faded away.

Kris Wu's killer was escaping!

The car screeched to a halt inches from Big Dan's uncle's wounded Buick. It had fresh bullet holes in it from the latest shots exchanged and a taillight had gone. Big Dan was not going to be happy.

Another car arrived, and another, and when Patricia looked up, she saw how much trouble they were in.

It was the Fou Chin Clan.

'Get them up,' commanded the harsh voice of Mr Yibo.

The women were already trying to get to their feet, Chelsea and Barbie both giving Miss May a helping hand when the Chinese gang members started grabbing them.

'Okay, okay,' Miss May protested. 'I'm doing it already.'

The five women were hauled to their feet and grabbed roughly by their arms so they faced the Fou Chin leader.

'Where is my marker?' Mr Yibo demanded.

Feeling indignant, Miss May said, 'You lied to us. You claimed Kris Wu stole it from you. The money was stolen from the Shenyang family, wasn't it?'

'It is of no consequence,' Yibo snapped.

Patricia argued. 'I think maybe it is. I think the Shenyang family are the big players here and that means you are either trying to curry favour by recovering it for them …' Patricia watched his eyes to see how he reacted, 'or you are in trouble and trying to fix the situation you find yourself in.'

Mr Yibo's eyes twitched, annoyance or possibly fear flitting across his face.

'I think we struck a nerve,' Chelsea saw the man react too. 'He's in trouble.'

'Kris Wu was one of yours,' Miss May stated. 'He stole twenty million from the Shenyang family and now you have to get it back to them before they exact retribution on you.'

Rage filled Yibo's face. He didn't need to admit it for the women to know they were right.

'Hey!' the new voice came from the mouth of the alley and all heads turned to see Wolf standing exposed in the open. Seeing the cars pull into the alley just after the women, he'd chosen to investigate.

Yibo twitched his head. 'Kill him,' he sneered.

The nearest two thugs spun around, bringing their assault rifles up already firing. There was no one there by the time their bullets reached the alley mouth, Wolf had already ducked back into cover behind the building.

'What about the dames, boss?' asked the man pinning Teeny's arms to her sides.

Yibo shot the women an angry glare. 'Leave them. They mean nothing.'

Abandoned in the alley, the women got to watch as Mr Yibo and the Fou Chin Clan ran for their cars.

'Where are we going?' the thug wanted to know.

'Freddie Lee's!' Shouted Mr Yibo. 'If whoever that was has the marker, he will be trying to get there as fast as possible. We have no time to lose!'

'We have to go too!' Chelsea ran for the Buick. 'We don't have the marker and if Kris Wu's killer gets away, we have nothing at all.'

'I'm never running again,' huffed Miss May, hurrying back toward the car but barely able to believe the pace of events or that they were entertaining chasing the armed Chinese criminals.

The Fou Chin were already leaving, their cars bursting from the far end of the alley to arrive back on Stanton Street with their tires slewing road dirt and their engines racing.

Chelsea dropped back into the driver's seat of Big Dan's uncle's once immaculate car. The Buick was leaning to one side now, the driver's door mirror was missing, a stray bullet leaving behind nothing but a jagged piece of metal where the mirror had once mounted, but the engine ran when she turned the key.

It became a straight up race. They had to get to Freddie Lee's before the man with the marker could exchange it for the money and vanish. They also had to avoid getting killed by the Fou Chin clan, the man with the marker, or anyone else that turned up for the party.

Things were tense in the Buick. Terror and adrenalin powered their pulses - none of them wanted to do what they were doing, and each held separate fears for how the next few minutes might play out, but they believed their only chance to get Bobbie and Petey out now was to catch the unknown player before anyone else could kill him or he could escape with the money.

On the backseat of the ruined car, Miss May and Patricia were busy discussing what they had seen and what it could mean. They had met the killer and the man revealed that Kris Wu knew him.

'He said Kris believed all the lies he ever told him,' Miss May recited the unknown player's words.

'That might have allowed him to get close,' commented Patricia. 'I bet Kris thought it was a friendly face approaching him.'

'Worse than that,' argued Miss May. 'I wouldn't be surprised if he convinced Kris to leave the Orange Banana Bar with him. Kris must have thought he was saved, but the man was leading him to his death.'

Patricia gave Miss May a meaningful look. 'I think I know who it might be.'

Miss May met her eyes. 'Me too. He's all by himself.'

'Exactly,' Patricia agreed.

'Who?' demanded Chelsea from the driver's seat, 'Who is he?'

'Yeah, who?' Teeny, sandwiched between the two sleuths, voiced her curiosity too. 'I feel more behind than usual.'

Barbie twisted in the front passenger seat to thump her friend's arm. 'Patty you are always doing this. Tell me what you know or so help me …'

'Everybody, hold onto your horses!' yelled Chelsea. They were back at Elizabeth Street where they would find the haberdashery and surely Kris Wu's killer. She cranked the steering wheel hard to the left, sliding the car around a tight bend in a manner the car was never designed to endure. Fighting hard to keep the rear car of the Fou Chin Clan in her sight, she'd pushed the car to its limits.

As she fought the wheel and the passengers all found themselves thrown against the opposite side of the car, something went clang and Chelsea lost control.

'Waaaaaaahhh!' Chelsea screamed as the steering wheel lost all resistance and simply spun in her hands. It was no longer connected to anything!

Her thoughts on the matter were echoed by the passengers, each finding their own preferred pitch in which to scream.

Mercifully, the brakes still worked, and Chelsea was able to bring the car to a stop before it mounted the kerb and slammed into a building. The giant car's back end slid around, bringing them broadside into the middle of the road.

They were back in Elizabeth Street, the haberdashery just fifty yards ahead of them where the Fou Chin's cars were now parked.

The Fou Chin were not getting out though, and from their position in the car, the ladies could see why.

The Tianjin Clan led by Vera Wong were back. Her emerald-green coat ruffled in the light breeze, so too her hair, but none of that caught the eye because her intense angry stare was all captivating. Spread out to her left and right just like before, were her besuited men. Except now, half of them were sporting white bandages and several looked to be in pain and struggling to stand. The other, very noticeable, difference was the machine pistols they carried in place of their hatchets.

They meant business.

'I want that marker!' shouted Vera Wong, her words aimed at the Fou Chin Clan.

The rear door of Mr Yibo's Bentley opened, and he stepped out.

'I do not have the marker,' he replied.

'Liar!' she screamed, her face contorting with rage. 'Why are you here if you do not have it?' Her troops all raised their guns.

Mr Yibo's calm exterior cracked. She had the drop on him. If her men started firing, they would cut his gang to pieces before they could get out of their cars or reverse out of the way.

'Another man has the marker,' he insisted, irritation evident in his voice. 'While you corner me, he is exchanging it for the stolen Shenyang money. Join with me and we can return it together.'

'Return it?' laughed Vera Wong. 'I am going to keep it. The Shenyang are not going to seize control of New York.'

In the Buick, Chelsea realised no one was going anywhere because the broken car they were in blocked the escape route.

'We have to get out of here,' she murmured.

Sitting next to her, Barbie agreed. 'Chelsea is right. This is a tinderbox. One false move and there could be bullets flying everywhere.'

The women grabbed door handles, poised to get out, and would have done so had the mouth of the street behind them not suddenly filled with bodies.

'Oh, God, who are these guys?' wailed Teeny. 'Pine Grove murders are so much more peaceful than this!'

Miss May gulped. 'At a guess, I would say they are the Shenyang.'

Her stab in the dark proved to be on the money and both the Fou Chin and Tianjin gangs had frozen to the spot.

There had to be close to a hundred members of the Shenyang family blocking the road. They filled it from side to side and were three deep in places. They were all armed and Patricia picked out two men who had chased them at Grand Central a few hours ago.

The women in Big Dan's uncle's car were hopelessly trapped.

'You wish to keep my money, do you?' a voice rang out from the centre of the Shenyang, drawing eyes toward the diminutive figure of an old man. Like an archetypal Chinese master, his facial hair was long and almost white, trailing from his chin and beneath his nose to form a long beard. He wore a suit, and on his feet were sandals.

There could be no doubt he led the Shenyang family and was its patriarch.

'You think we are not able to take control of this city?' he questioned, his eyes invisible in the dark but undoubtedly staring straight at Vera Wong.

On the spot and too late to retract her words, the head of the Tianjin gang had little choice but to fight. She was outnumbered, but where the Shenyang were exposed, her troops had the option of cover to their left and right, plus the Fou Chin Clan were smack in the middle between the two opposing factions – they were the ones in real danger if the shooting started.

Unwilling to wait to see who started shooting, Patricia shoved her door open.

'Wait!' she begged.

The street became a frozen tableau. In the window of the Haberdashery, Tommy's giant tattooed face could be seen peeking out from between rolls of material. The Fou Chin, Vera Wong's men, and the Shenyang were all staring at the out of place woman with the English accent.

Another door opened and Miss May clambered out of the ailing car to join her new friend.

'Yes, please wait,' she begged. 'You have all been misled.'

'Kris Wu was informing on you,' Patricia tried to get her words out quickly, unsure how long they could keep the street full of gun-toting killers from shooting everything and everyone in sight. 'He was under the wing of an FBI agent called Hu Chang.'

'What does this have to do with my money?' demanded the aged Shenyang patriarch.

'Kris Wu stole it because he believed you knew he was informing on you. He believed you were going to kill him, and he chose to flee.'

'A wise move,' agreed the Shenyang patriarch.

Miss May took up the narrative. 'But he wasn't in any danger. None of you knew what he was doing, did you?'

The silence in the street told a story more clearly than words.

Patricia nodded – they had this part right and that meant they had most likely figured it all out.

'Kris Wu took your money because he planned to escape, but it wasn't his idea. The seed had been sown by someone else. When he heard that Agent Chang had gone missing, he assumed you had caught him and that he was dead. The logical conclusion following that was that Agent Chang would have given up Kris Wu's name and he had to run.'

'Again, a logical conclusion,' agreed the patriarch. 'However, I have never heard of an Agent Chang.'

He confirmed what Miss May and Patricia believed and the final piece of the puzzle slotted into place.

Mr Yibo could contain his curiosity no longer. 'Who killed Kris Wu?' he demanded to know.

Miss May looked at Patricia who inclined her head. Miss May said, 'Agent Chang.'

The silence in the street was absolute.

Vera Wong frowned in her misunderstanding. 'But you said he was dead,' she pointed out as if the two sleuths might have missed that vital fact.

Barbie slipped from the confines of the car to join Miss May and Patricia in the street. It was partly because the car was never going to move again, and thus made for a poor means of escape, and partly because she could hear the rumble of large engines in the distance. It was faint, but it was also getting closer.

Miss May turned her head to look at Vera Wong. 'What I said was that Kris Wu assumed Agent Chang was dead. Agent Chang did not have the connections to steal the money. He needed someone on the inside for that, someone who could get to it ... which is why he targeted Kris Wu. Kris Wu's family is on their way to America. They're due to arrive tomorrow.'

'So this Agent Chang stole the money?' Mr Yibo attempted to confirm, his brain unable to wade through the confusion.

The patriarch sighed. 'No, Yibo, you imbecile. Agent Chang ensured Kris Wu would do it when triggered. He made Wu believe his life was in danger from us by faking his own death. Wu grabbed the money when he made the drug drop to us yesterday afternoon. We were looking for him, but he stashed the money with Freddie Lee and with the marker in his possession, he attempted to hide. We found him, but by then he was already dead.'

'So who killed him?' Vera Wong wanted to know.

Patricia supplied the answer before anyone else could. 'Agent Chang. He's in Freddie Lee's right now. Or, at least, he was. I would imagine he has taken the money and fled already.'

What happened next was difficult to recall. Who shot first, the order in which events played out, would be argued by all the surviving participants but never agreed upon.

The only thing they knew for certain was that the police chose that moment to spring their trap and the world went up in smoke.

Two bright floodlights, erected in secret just an hour ago high above the street on the roofs of the buildings on either side, flashed into life. The sudden intense light stunned everyone as SWAT units converged from both ends of the street.

The on-scene commander, a woman named McNamara, had Captain Mainwaring at her side. He'd provided all the intel and got the units into place. It was a hunch, but one which paid off.

Half the Chinese organised crime gangs in New York were likely to be in a single place at the same time. They were exposed and they were committing a crime carrying weapons in the street. The police waited for someone to admit to something more, which the Shenyang patriarch just had in talking about drug shipments. They were ready to pounce but there were five civilian women in the way.

Mainwaring wanted to wait; McNamara overruled him. The chance of the ladies escaping alive was so slim, she calculated, and the chance for the criminals to escape too great, for her to hesitate in the moment of glory.

At street level, it took half a second for the Chinese gangs to realise they had been lured into a trap. Their only choice was to shoot their way out.

Vera Wong saw an opportunity to remove the head of the Shenyang family and Yibo saw a chance to wet his pants. As people started shooting and running, he threw himself to the ground and crawled under his car.

The SWAT teams fired tear gas into the crowd. The Chinese gangsters were dispersing anyway, trying to find a way out of the street. Several bolted for Freddie Lee's haberdashery, darting inside without resistance from Tommy because he had already gone out the back door and was doing his best to blend into the late-night pedestrian traffic.

Barbie and Chelsea were holding hands, the two women gripping each other tightly amid the terror ensuing around them. However, most of the bullets were being fired outwards at the cops, placing the women in the eye of the storm, so to speak.

When smoke began to fill the street, they saw their chance and screamed for their friends to follow. In a mad dash for cover, the five women ran headlong into Freddie Lee's shop. Half the windows were missing, and fires had started where stray bullets caused material to smoulder and ignite.

They ran through the shop, weaving along like a crocodile, all holding hands in a long line. They passed Freddie's desk, seeing the ledger was gone along with Freddie, and they pushed on through the building until they found a back door. Exiting into a moonlit courtyard behind the shop, they sucked in clean cool air and thanked their lucky stars to still be in one piece.

Back in Elizabeth Street the firing slowed and petered out. Apart from the few who escaped through the haberdashery, the Chinese gangs vying for control had either killed each other or been cut down by the police when they tried to resist. Now the police were moving in to mop up those who remained.

In McNamara's report, it would be recorded as a textbook operation. From her vantage point above, she'd seen the civilians escape and no civilian casualties meant she was in for a commendation for sure.

Getting her breath back, Teeny asked, 'What about the money and Kris Wu's killer? We didn't get either. How are we going to get Petey and his friend out now? Break 'em out with our bare hands?'

Chelsea sighed. 'Teeny's right. We still have no evidence to prove they didn't kill Kris Wu. Agent Chang, I assume it was he who took the marker from us, has the money and can vanish into the wind.'

Barbie lifted her hand. 'He doesn't have the money,' she announced boldly. Opening her fingers, she revealed the marker lying flat on her palm.

Teeny's brow creased. 'But we saw you give it to him in the alley behind the biker bar.'

Patricia burst out laughing, the sound sudden and shocking in the quiet courtyard. 'You switched it! You gave him the one we got from the waitress, didn't you?'

'Might have,' grinned Barbie.

'I think I'll take that,' announced Agent Chang as he appeared from the other side of the courtyard with his right arm raised and a gun pointed at the women yet again.

All five women spun around to face the latest threat, gasping in shock and surprise to see Kris Wu's killer lying in wait for them.

Halfway to them, his pace faltered. The roar of large engines had been growing louder for the last few minutes and now it filled the air as motorcycles swept into the courtyard. Biker after biker rode straight at Agent Chang, Wolf in the lead astride a giant chrome-covered chopper.

Agent Chang swivelled on his toes but couldn't get the gun facing the right way in time to prevent Wolf from hitting him.

The wayward FBI agent flew up and back, blasted from his feet by almost a thousand pounds of man and machine. With a fist raised to head height, Wolf called his motorcycle club to a halt.

Patricia, Miss May, Teeny, Barbie, and Chelsea were all staring slack-jawed and open-mouthed at the mass of bikes and men, and the battered form of FBI Agent Chang.

Sprawled on the ground, Chang wasn't dead. He wasn't even unconscious for he was trying to get up. It was, however, clear that he had been injured. Wolf sent men to remove his weapon and crossed the courtyard to get to Barbie and her friends.

'I'm sorry I couldn't get here sooner, Barbie,' he purred in his deep bass voice and held her gaze with his own.

'Oh, come on,' complained Chelsea. 'Get a room.'

SWAT were clearing through the haberdashery behind them, urgent commands being shouted back and forth to make it clear they had total command of the area and the situation.

They burst from the back of the building a moment later, excitement and adrenalin driving them to round up all the ladies and the bikers until they could sort out who was who.

Captain Mainwaring arrived less than a minute after the SWAT team, clarifying who the women were and ensuring they were left alone.

'Lieutenant Danvers came out of surgery and regained consciousness,' he revealed. 'He's going to be fine, but he insisted they find him a phone so he could call me. It seems I treated you harshly earlier. Your story checks out. Now, can you please tell me what is going on?'

As the controlled bedlam happened around them, the five women couldn't help but exchange tired smiles. It was done.

They explained about Agent Chang, pointing out the broken form receiving treatment from two paramedics just a few yards away, and they regaled the police captain with the story of Kris Wu and how they perceived events occurred the previous evening.

There was, however, one vital piece of information they left out.

Riding Pillion

Wolf insisted on waiting until the police told the ladies they were free to go. Barbie, Chelsea, and everyone else wanted to go straight back to the police station, however Bobbie and Petey would not be processed and released until the morning – according to Captain Mainwaring it wasn't as simple as just opening the cell door and waving them goodbye because they were innocent.

The women were too tired to argue.

The girls from Pine Grove never had gotten around to organising a place to stay that night. After arranging to have Big Dan's uncle's car towed away – not that there was much left of it - they were only too pleased to accompany Barbie and Patricia back to their hotel.

'Won't it be tight quarters?' asked Teeny before they set off. 'I mean, I'm small, but I sleep like Hulk Hogan.'

Patricia didn't bother to explain in detail, she just assured Teeny there would be enough room. The presidential suite at the Credenza had five bedrooms and a private swimming pool. They were not going to be squeezed in like sardines.

The doorman at the Credenza had a startled expression and wide, wide eyes when the rumble of motorcycles coming his way turned off the road to swing under the hotel's grand front façade.

Riding pillion behind Wolf and four of his other bikers, the five ladies arrived safely back at their hotel.

Chelsea, Miss May, Teeny, and Patricia moved to one side, politely thanking those they had ridden with, then waited for Barbie.

Still astride his bike, Wolf hit Barbie with smouldering eyes when he said, 'If you are ever back in New York …'

Barbie offered him a lopsided smile. 'I have a boyfriend. It's kind of serious.' She made it sound like an apology.

Wolf nodded, his own smile one of regretful acceptance. 'We miss every shot we don't take, Barbie. I wish you health and happiness. And … if you are ever back in New York …'

Barbie leaned down to plant a gentle kiss on the man's cheek and whispered, 'Thank you.'

'The motorcycle club has a new tale to tell, one where we rode to the rescue of a beautiful woman and her friends.'

Chelsea rolled her eyes.

Wolf raised his right fist again, signalling that it was time to go. The engine noise increased as they pulled away never once looking back.

Teeny said it, 'That is one cool, sexy man. He's no Big Dan, of course. But he is … something else.'

Epilogue

'Tell me again what we are doing here,' requested Petey.

The cold breeze and moist air coming off the Hudson River were making him want to be anywhere else. Preferably somewhere far away from New York and inside where it was warm. He was fantasising about eating every berry pie with a scoop of ice cream back in Pine Grove.

'It's okay, brah,' drawled Bobbie, thumping a comradely fist against Petey's shoulder. 'We are free, brah. I don't care what we do today, I am going to savour the sweet air and enjoy it.'

Barbie leaned into her younger brother, glad to know he was safe again and they all watched the people filing through the port.

Zhou Li, the young waitress they met the previous evening, had been surprised to receive their call late last night. They caught her just as the restaurant was shutting. Realising who she was talking to, Zhou had jabbered on about all that had allegedly happened.

According to her, there had been some insane shootout between several of the Chinese gangs and the cops and Freddie Lee's place had gone up in smoke!

All five women were crowded around the phone in Patricia's sumptuous suite. They were tired but there was a final piece of business to which they had to attend. If they wanted to go home the next day, it really couldn't wait.

They all agreed this was the right thing to do.

Zhou Li stood at the exit to the port, a sign in her hands written in both Chinese and English which simply read 'Liu Wu'.

Several times they thought perhaps the woman exiting with a small child might be the dead man's wife, but on each occasion, they saw the waitress ask a question and receive a head shake in reply.

Eventually though, her question got a surprised look from a woman holding a small baby.

'That's her,' said Miss May with a smile.

'This is a good thing,' agreed Patricia, pleased they were one voice on the subject.

Zhou Li handed Liu Wu the letter from her husband. It had been carefully resealed and now contained the marker worth twenty million dollars.

Arriving in America, Liu Wu was about to discover her husband was dead, but Freddie Lee still had the money and would set up shop somewhere else very soon. Zhou Li was going to ensure Kris Wu's widow was given lodging and help as she adjusted, and whether she went back to China or stayed in the States, she was a rich woman now.

It might not be all that she wanted, but life would go on and her daughter's future would be secure.

As Zhou Li began to lead Liu Wu away from the port, Patricia, Miss May, and all the others turned away, satisfied they had done all they could.

'How soon is your flight?' asked Miss May.

Patricia checked her watch. 'We need to check in two hours from now. We fly at two o'clock.'

Miss May pursed her lips. 'Time for a gin?'

The End

Author's notes by Steve Higgs

Hello, Dear Readers,

Thank you for finishing this fun series crossover story. I shall assume, since you are still reading, that you enjoyed it enough to not want it to end. If that is the case, I have a whole pot of good news for you.

I'll circle back to that shortly.

First, I feel it time I explained a few of my quirky Englishisms.

In the bar, when they get to know each other, the ladies call stumps on drinking any more gin. I worry that this is a particularly English term and will make no sense in some other territories. It comes from cricket where at the end of play, the umpire signals lunch or tea by removing the stumps (the bit the bowler is trying to knock over and the batsman is defending).

The names for parts of a car is also a fun discussion. Almost every part of a standard car has a different name in America when compared to Great Britain. Hood and trunk are bonnet and boot for a start. Posted close to a US infantry regiment a few decades ago when I was still a soldier, I learned all about the surprising differences in our shared language.

I'm sure there are people who wonder how a joint story like this comes about. It went a little like this.

If you have come to discover me through your love of Chelsea Thomas, you are a person of refined taste and should commend yourself on your selection of reading material. I came to know Chelsea through mutual membership of an independent author group. Through many conversations in which we supported and helped each other through our growing author careers, we came to see many similarities in not just our stories, but also our characters.

If you ever choose to examine the cozy mystery charts on Amazon, you will find Chelsea Thomas's books right alongside mine and generally sitting among the top few titles.

I do not recall which of us first suggested sticking them all together for an adventure, but the result was more fun than I could have hoped for. There may well be more joint stories to come.

If you are new to me, I will tell you that as of July 2021 (present time for me as I write this note) I have sixty separate titles published across five different series, all of which are intertwined. Patricia and Barbie appear in a third of them, but their story is far from over and more books will come yet.

Those readers who arrived at this point because they follow me, ought to scroll down (or turn the pages) to find the links/advertisement for Chelsea Thomas's Apple Orchard series. I have read them. They are great.

The pot of good news is that Chelsea has a stack of books for you to investigate. The Apple Orchard series is thirteen books deep already and that is not the only series the author has published.

Take care.

Steve Higgs

Apple Orchard Cozy Mystery by Chelsea Thomas

APPLE ORCHARD COZY MYSTERY BOOK 1

Apple Die

CHELSEA THOMAS

Everyone adores Miss May ... except the guilty.

In a small town, where neighbors know each other, lawn chairs come out in the spring, and if you sit around chatting long enough, someone brings you pie, there are still skeletons in every closet. Luckily for Pine Grove, Miss May has a nose for crime.

The body was found face-down in the orchard.

Chelsea's not sure crime-fighting is her strong suit. She's up at her Aunt May's farm recovering from heartbreak, after all, trying to forget the guy who left her at the altar. But when cousin Maggie's fiancé is murdered, Chelsea's own botched wedding seems like less of a big deal.

Who would have killed him?

The handsome and charming Detective Wayne thinks it's Maggie. Miss May and Chelsea know he's wrong, but they don't have proof. There's a killer on the loose in their little town and they're determined to find the culprit.

You'll adore this apple orchard cozy because everyone loves small-town mysteries with comedy, suspense and yummy food.

More Books by Steve Higgs
Blue Moon Investigations

Paranormal Nonsense

The Phantom of Barker Mill

Amanda Harper Paranormal Detective

The Klowns of Kent

Dead Pirates of Cawsand

In the Doodoo With Voodoo

The Witches of East Malling

Crop Circles, Cows and Crazy Aliens

Whispers in the Rigging

Bloodlust Blonde – a short story

Paws of the Yeti

Under a Blue Moon – A Paranormal Detective Origin Story

Night Work

Lord Hale's Monster

The Herne Bay Howlers

Undead Incorporated

The Ghoul of Christmas Past

The Sandman
Jailhouse Golem
Sparks in the Darkness
Shadow in the Mine

Patricia Fisher Cruise Mysteries
The Missing Sapphire of Zangrabar
The Kidnapped Bride
The Director's Cut
The Couple in Cabin 2124
Doctor Death
Murder on the Dancefloor
Mission for the Maharaja
A Sleuth and her Dachshund in Athens
The Maltese Parrot
No Place Like Home

Patricia Fisher Mystery Adventures
What Sam Knew
Solstice Goat
Recipe for Murder
A Banshee and a Bookshop
Diamonds, Dinner Jackets, and Death
Frozen Vengeance
Mug Shot
The Godmother
Murder is an Artform
Wonderful Weddings and Deadly Divorces
Dangerous Creatures

Patricia Fisher: Ship's Detective

Patricia Fisher: Ship's Detective

Albert Smith Culinary Capers
Pork Pie Pandemonium
Bakewell Tart Bludgeoning
Stilton Slaughter
Bedfordshire Clanger Calamity
Death of a Yorkshire Pudding
Cumberland Sausage Shocker
Arbroath Smokie Slaying
Dundee Cake Dispatch
Lancashire Hotpot Peril
Blackpool Rock Bloodshed

Felicity Philips Investigates
To Love and to Perish
Tying the Noose
Aisle Kill Him
A Dress to Die for

Real of False Gods
Untethered magic
Unleashed Magic
Early Shift
Damaged but Powerful
Demon Bound
Familiar Territory
The Armour of God

Free Books and More

Get sneak peaks, exclusive giveaways, behind the scenes content, and more. Plus, you'll be notified of Fan Pricing events when they occur and get exclusive offers from other authors because all UF writers are automatically friends.

Not only that, but you'll receive an exclusive FREE story staring Otto and Zachary and two free stories from the author's Blue Moon Investigations series.

Yes, please! Sign me up for lots of FREE stuff and bargains!

Want to follow me and keep up with what I am doing?

Facebook

Printed in Great Britain
by Amazon